"Your sister is a pretty fair singer too, you know," he drawled. "How *did* you miss that gene?"

Hannah shook the cotton wool from her head. "*That's* what you came over here to say? Not, *Are you having a good time, Hannah?* Or, *Can I get you another drink, Hannah?* But, *What's with the talent deficiency?* You are a charmer."

He laughed softly, a low rumble that whispered to all the deep, dark feminine places inside of her. Serious face on, he was heart-stoppingly gorgeous. Smiling, he was devastating. Laughing, he was...a dream.

This man had been hitting on her? Her? Sensible, back-chatting, small-town Hannah Gillespie? She felt it, but couldn't quite believe it.

When **ALLY BLAKE** was a little girl, she made a wish that when she turned twenty-six she would marry an Italian two years older than herself. After it actually came true, she realized she was onto something with these wish things. So, next she wished that she could make a living spending her days in her pajamas, eating M&M's and drinking scads of coffee while using her formative experiences of wallowing in teenage crushes and romantic movies to create love stories of her own. The fact that she is now able to spend her spare time searching the internet for pictures of handsome guys for research purposes is merely a bonus!

Come along and visit her website at www.allyblake.com.

THE ROGUE
WEDDING GUEST

ALLY BLAKE

~ IN BED WITH THE BOSS ~

Harlequin®

TORONTO NEW YORK LONDON
AMSTERDAM PARIS SYDNEY HAMBURG
STOCKHOLM ATHENS TOKYO MILAN MADRID
PRAGUE WARSAW BUDAPEST AUCKLAND

Recycling programs
for this product may
not exist in your area.

ISBN-13: 978-0-373-52816-5

THE ROGUE WEDDING GUEST
Previously published in the U.K. as THE WEDDING DATE

First North American Publication 2011

THE ROGUE
WEDDING GUEST

This one's for white chocolate
raspberry muffins and macadamia choc chip
cookies. Or more specifically, the fab staff
at my fave local cafés who let me
write this book in their welcoming warmth
and know my order by heart.

CHAPTER ONE

'You're him! Aren't you?'

The gorgeous specimen of manhood in the dark sunglasses, at the pointy end of a squat pale pink fingernail, sat stock still. To the eclectic, late-afternoon Brunswick Street crowd rushing past the sidewalk café he would have appeared simply cool. Collected. Quietly attentive behind a half-smile so effortlessly sexy it could stop traffic. Literally.

Hannah knew better.

Hannah, who worked harder and with longer hours than anyone else she knew, would have bet her precious life savings on the fact that, behind those ubiquitous dark sunglasses he was hoping, almost desperately, that the older woman on the other end of the finger might quickly realise she had mistaken him for someone else.

No such luck.

'You are!' the woman continued, flat feet planted determinedly on the uneven cobbled ground. 'I know you are! You're the guy who makes that *Voyagers* TV show. I've seen you in magazines. And on the telly. My daughter just *loooves* you. She even considered going into training once, so she could be one of those regular-type people you send off into the wild and up mountains with nothing but a toothbrush and a packet of Tim-Tams. Or however it goes. And that's saying something! It's all but impossible to get that girl off the couch.

You know what? I should give you her number. She's quite pretty in her way, and unquestionably single…'

Sitting—with apparently Ninja-like invisibility—on the other side of the rickety table that served as Knight Productions' office those times when the boss felt the need to get out of the confines of their manic headquarters, Hannah had to cover her mouth to smother the laugh threatening to bubble to the surface.

Any other time of day or night her boss was like the mountains he had so famously conquered before turning his attentions to encouraging others to do the same on TV. He was colossal, tough, unyielding, indomitable, enigmatic. Which was why seeing him wriggle and squirm and practically lose the power of speech under the attentions of an overtly loving fan was always a moment to relish.

It had taken Hannah less than half a day of the year she'd worked for Bradley Knight to realise that overt adoration was her boss's Achilles' heel. Awards, industry accolades, gushing peers, bowing and scraping minions—all turned him to stone.

And then there were the fans. The many, many, *many* fans who knew a good thing when they saw it. And there was no denying that Bradley Knight was six feet four inches of very good thing.

Just like that, the laughter tickling Hannah's throat turned into a small, uncomfortable lump.

She frowned deeply, cleared her throat, and shifted on her wrought-iron seat, redistributing the balance of her buttocks. And more importantly her train of thought.

The very last thing her boss needed was even the smallest clue that in moments of overworked, overtired weakness he'd even given *her* the occasional tummy-flutter. And sweaty palms. And hot flushes. And raging fantasies the likes of which she wouldn't dare share with even her best friend, whose good-natured ribbing about Hannah's constant proximity to their gorgeous boss had come all too close to hitting the mark on a number of occasions.

The beep of a car horn split the air, and Hannah flinched out of her heady daydream to find herself breathing a little too heavily and staring moonily at her boss.

Hannah frowned so hard she pulled a muscle in her neck.

She'd worked her backside off to get there, to take any job she could get in order to gain experience before finally finding the one she loved. The one she was really good at. The one she was meant to do. And she wasn't going to do anything to risk that career path now.

Even if that wasn't reason enough, pining after the guy was a complete a waste of time. He was a rock. He'd never let her in. He never let *anyone* in. And when it came to relationships Hannah wasn't prepared to accept anything less than *wonderful*.

Don't. Ever. Forget it.

She glanced at her watch. It was nearly four. Phew. The long weekend looming ahead of her—four days away from her all-consuming job and her all-consuming boss—clearly could not have come at a better time.

Still on the clock, she turned her concentration back to the woman who might as well have had her boss at knife-point he was sitting so eerily still.

She scraped her chair back and intervened, before Bradley managed to perform the first ever case of human osmosis and disappeared through the holes in his wrought-iron chair.

The woman only noticed her existence when Hannah slung an arm around her shoulders and none too gently eased her to the kerb.

'Do you know him?' the woman asked, breathless.

Glancing back at Bradley, Hannah felt her inner imp take over. Leaning in, she murmured, 'I've seen the inside of his fridge. It's frighteningly clean.'

The woman's still glittering eyes widened, and she finally focussed fully on Hannah. She was very thorough in her perusal of the kinks that always managed to appear in Hannah's straightened hair by that time of the afternoon. The countless creases in her designer dress. The chunky man's diving watch hanging loosely around her thin wrist. The cowboy boots poking out from beneath it all.

Then the woman smiled.

With a none too comfortable flash of realisation it hit Hannah that she was being compared unfavourably to the daughter who never got off the couch. Her inner imp limped back into hiding.

Eight hours earlier she'd looked the epitome of personal assistant to Australia's most successful television producer— even despite the little odes to her tomboy roots. You could take the girl out of small-town Tasmania, but...

But she didn't say any of that. With a shrug she admitted, 'I'm Mr Knight's personal assistant.'

'Oh.' The woman nodded, as if that made so much more sense than a man like him *choosing* to spend time with her— because when he said jump, she knew how high without even having to ask.

After a little more chat, Hannah turned the woman in the opposite direction, gave her a little push and waved goodbye as, like a zombie, she trudged away down the street.

She brushed off her hands. Another job well done. Then she turned, hands on hips, to find Bradley running long fingers beneath his eyes, sliding his sunglasses almost high enough to offer a teasing glimpse of the arresting silvery-grey eyes beneath. But not quite.

Then slowly, achingly slowly, his rigid body began to unclench. Muscle by hard-earned muscle, limb by long, strong limb, down his considerable length until his legs slid under the table and his large shoes poked lazily out at the other side.

The apparent languor was all an act. The effort of a private man to restrain whatever it was that drew people to him like moths to a flame. Unfortunately for him it only made the restrained power seething inside him more obvious. More compelling. A familiar sweep of sensation skipped blithely across her skin again—a soft, melty, pulsing feeling.

Even the fact that she knew *she* was about to bear the brunt of the dark mood he'd be in after the one-way love-in didn't make her immune.

At least it hadn't yet.

Time was what she needed. Time and space, so that the boundaries of her life weren't defined by the monstrous number of hours she spent deep inside Bradley's overwhelming creative vision. Thanks heavens for the long weekend!

Actually, time, space *and* meeting a guy would do it for sure. A guy who might actually stand a chance in hell of feeling that way about her.

He was out there. Somewhere. She was sure of it. He had to be. Because she absolutely wasn't going to settle for anything less than everything. She'd seen first-hand what 'settling' looked like in the first of the three marriages her mother had leapt into after her father passed away. It wasn't pretty. In fact it was downright sordid. That wasn't going to be her life.

She blinked as her boss's beautifully chiselled face came into such sharp focus her breath caught in her throat. He was something. But any woman who hoped in Bradley Knight's direction was asking for heartache. Many had tried. Many more yet would. But nobody on earth would topple that mountain.

She grabbed the wayward swathe of hair flickering across her face and tucked it behind her ear, plastered a smile across her face, and bounded back to the table. Bradley didn't look up. Didn't even flicker a lash. He probably hadn't even realised she'd left.

'Wasn't she a lovely lady?' Hannah sing-songed. 'We're sending her daughter a signed copy of last season's *Voyagers*.'

'Why me?' Bradley asked, still looking into the distance.

She knew he wasn't talking about posting a DVD. 'You were just born lucky,' she said wryly.

'You think I'm lucky?' he asked.

'Ooh, yeah. Fairies sprinkled fortune dust on your cradle as you slept. Why else do you think you've been so ridiculously successful at everything you've ever set your heart on?'

His head swung her way. Even with the dark sunglasses between them, the force of his undivided attention was like a thunderclap. Her heart-rate quadrupled in response.

His voice was a touch deeper when he said, 'So, in your eyes, my life has nothing to do with hard work, persistence, and knowing just enough about man's primal need to prove himself as a man?'

Hannah tapped a finger on her chin and took a few seconds to damp down her own latent needs as she looked up at the cloudy blue sky. Then she said, 'Nah.'

The appreciative rumble of his laughter danced across her nerves, creating a whole new wave of warmth cascading through her. Enjoying him from the other side of the mile-high walls he wore like a second skin was imprudent enough. Enduring the bombardment of his personal attention was a whole other battle.

'If you really want to know why you are so lucky, give that lady's daughter a call. Take her to dinner. Ask her yourself.' She waved the piece of paper with the woman's address and phone number on it. 'Talk about a PR windfall. "Bradley Knight dates fan. Falls in love. Moves to suburbs. Coaches little league team. Learns to cook lamb roast."'

She could sense his eyes narrowing behind his sunglasses. He then took his sweet time sitting upright. He managed to make the move appear leisurely—inconsequential, even—but the constrained power pulsing through every limb, every digit, every hair was patently clear to anyone with half an instinct. She could feel the blood pumping through her veins.

'At this moment,' he said, his voice a deep, dark warning, 'I am so very, very glad you are my assistant and *not* in charge of PR.'

Hannah slid the paper into her overstuffed leather diary and said, 'Yeah, me too. I'm not sure there's enough money in the world that could tempt me to take on a job whereby I'd have to spend my days trying to convince the world how wonderful you are. I mean, I work hard now—but come on…'

Frown lines appeared above his glasses as he leaned across the table till his forearms covered half the thing. He was so big he blocked out the sun—a massive shadow of a man, with a golden halo outlining his bulk.

Hannah's fingertips were within touching distance of his. She could feel every single hair on her arms stand to attention one by delicious one. Her feet were tucked so far under her chair—so as to not accidentally scrape against his—she was getting a cramp.

'Aren't we in a strange mood today?' he asked.

His voice was quiet, dropping so very low, and so very much only for her ears she felt it hum in the backs of her knees.

He tilted his chin in her direction. 'What gives?'

And then he slid his sunglasses from his eyes. Smoky grey they were—or quicksilver—entirely depending on his mood. In that moment they were so dark the colour was impenetrable.

The man was such a workaholic he never looked to her without a dozen instructions ready to be barked. But in that moment he just looked at her. And waited. Hannah's throat turned to ash.

'What gives,' another voice shot back, 'is that our Hannah's mind is already turned to a weekend of debauchery and certain nookie.'

Hannah flinched so hard at the sudden intrusion she bit her lip.

Yet through the stinging pain, for a split second, she was almost sure she saw a flicker of something that looked a heck of a lot like disappointment flash across Bradley's face. Then his eyes lowered to her swollen lip, which she was lapping at with her tongue.

Then, as though she had been imagining the whole thing, he glanced away, leaned back, and turned to the owner of that last gem of a comment.

'Sonja,' he drawled. 'Nice of you to show up.'

'Pleasure,' Sonja said.

'Perfect timing,' Hannah added, her voice breathier than she would have hoped. 'Bradley was just about to offer me your job.'

Sonja didn't even flinch, but the flicker of amusement in Bradley's cheek made her feel warm all over. She shut down her smile before it took hold. Not only was Sonja Bradley's PR guru, she was also Hannah's flatmate. And the only reason she knew how to use a blowdryer and had access to the kind of non-jeans-and-T-shirt-type clothes that filled her closet.

Sonja perched her curvaceous self upon a chair and crossed her legs, her eyes never once leaving her iPhone as one black-taloned finger skipped ridiculously fast over the screen.

In fact her stillness gave Hannah a sudden chill. She clapped a hand over her friend's phone, and Sonja blinked as though coming round from a trance.

Hannah said, 'If you are even *thinking* of Tweeting any-thing about my upcoming weekend off and debauchery and nookie, or anything along those lines—even if I am named "anonymous Knight Productions staffer"—I will order a beet-root burger and drop it straight on this dress.'

Sonja's dark gaze narrowed and focussed on the cream wool of the dress Hannah had borrowed from her wardrobe. Slowly she slid her phone into a tiny crocodile skin purse.

'Why do I feel even more like I'm on the other side of the looking glass from you two than usual?'

Hannah and Sonja both turned to Bradley.

He looked ever so slightly pained as he said, 'I'm feeling like it's going to give me indigestion to even bring this up, but I can't *not* ask. Debauchery? Nookie?'

At the word 'debauchery' his eyes slid to Hannah—dark, smoke-grey, inscrutable—before sliding back to Sonja. It was only a fraction of a second. But a fraction was plenty long enough to take her breath clean away.

Boy, did she need a holiday. And *now!*

Sonja motioned for an espresso as she said, 'For an ostensibly smart man, if it doesn't involve you or your mountains, you have the memory of a sieve. This is the weekend our Hannah is heading back home to the delightful southern island of Tasmania, to play bridesmaid at her sister Elyse's wedding—which she organised.'

His eyes slid back to Hannah, and this time they stayed. 'That's *this* weekend?'

Hannah blinked at him. Slowly. She'd told him as much at least a dozen times in the past fortnight, yet it had clearly not sunk in. It was just what she needed in order to finally become completely unscrambled.

Sonja had been spot-on. Bradley had a one-track mind. And if something didn't serve him it didn't exist.

'I have the New Zealand trip this weekend,' he said.

'Yes, you do.' Hannah glanced at her watch. 'And I'm off the clock in ten minutes. Sonja? What are *your* plans?'

Sonja grinned from ear to ear at the sarcasm dripping from Hannah's words. 'I'll be sitting all alone in our little apartment, feeling supremely jealous. For this weekend you will have your absolute pick.'

'My pick of what?' Hannah asked.

Sonja leaned forward and looked her right in the eye. 'Oodles of gussied-up, aftershave-drenched men, bombarded by more concentrated romance than they can handle. They'll be walking around that wedding like wolves in heat. It's the most primal event you'll see in civilised society.'

With that, Sonja leant back, wiping an imaginary bead of sweat from her brow, before returning to texting up a storm.

Hannah sat stock still, feeling a mite warmer in the chilly Melbourne afternoon. Having insisted on planning her little sister's wedding in the spare minutes she had left each day, in a fit of guilt at being maid of honour from several hundred kilometres' distance, she'd been so absolutely swamped that the idea of a holiday fling had not once entered her mind.

Maybe a random red-hot weekend was exactly what she needed—to unwind, de-knot, take stock, recharge, and remember there was a whole wide world outside of Bradley Knight's orbit.

'The groomsmen will be top of the list, of course,' Sonja continued. 'But they'll be so ready for action it'll be embarrassing. Best you avoid them. My advice is to look out for another interstate guest—more mystery, and less likely to be a close relative. Or a fisherman.'

Hannah scoffed, and shut her eyes tight against Sonja's small-town-life bashing.

'You're on the pill, right?'

'Sonja!'

Really, that was a step too far. But she was. Not that she'd found cause to need it much of late. Her hours were prohibitive, and her work so consuming she was simply too exhausted to even remember why she'd gone on the pill in the first place.

But now she had four whole days in a beautiful resort, in the middle of a winter wonderland wilderness, surrounded by dozens of single guys. A small fire lit inside her stomach for the first time in the months since she'd known she was going home.

She was about to get herself a whole load of time, space, *and* the chance she might meet an actual guy. Heck, what were the chances she'd find The One back on the island from which she'd fled all those years ago?

When she opened an eye it was to find Bradley frowning. Though if it was about anything to do with her she'd eat her shoes.

She shoved the last of her papers into a large, heavy leather satchel. Her voice was firm as she said, 'I'm heading to the office now, to make sure Spencer has everything he needs in order to be me this weekend.'

'That's your replacement for a major location scout?' Bradley asked. 'The intern with the crush?'

Her hand turned into a fist inside the bag, and she glanced up at her boss. 'Spencer doesn't have a *crush* on me. He just wants to *be* me when he grows up.'

One dark eyebrow kicked north. 'The kid practically salivates every time you walk in the room.'

That he notices…?

'Then lucky for you. With me gone, you'll have a salivation-free weekend.'

'That's the positive?'

Hannah shrugged. 'Told you—I suck at PR. Lucky for me I'm so good at my actual job you are clearly pining in advance. In fact, it's so clear how much you'll miss me I'm thinking the time's ripe to ask for a promotion.'

It was a throwaway comment, but it seemed to hang there between them as if it had been shouted. His eyebrows flattened and his grey eyes clouded. Behind them was a coming storm. He reached distractedly across the table and stole the small sugar biscuit from the edge of Sonja's saucer.

Blithely changing the subject, he said, 'Four days.'

'Four days and enough pre-wedding functions you'd think they were royalty.' But, no, the bride was simply her mother's daughter. 'The wedding's on Sunday. I'll be back Tuesday morning.'

'Covered in hickies, no doubt,' Sonja threw in, most

helpfully. 'Her mother *was* Miss Tasmania, after all. Down there she's considered good breeding stock.'

Thank goodness at that moment Sonja spied someone with whom to schmooze. With a waving hand and a loud *'daaaarling'* she was gone, leaving Bradley and Hannah alone again.

Bradley was watching her quietly, and thanks to Sonja—who'd clearly been born without a discreet bone in her body—the swirl of sexual innuendo was ringing in her ears. Hannah felt as if all the air had been sapped from the sky.

'So you're heading home?' Bradley asked, voice low.

'Tomorrow morning. Even though last night I dreamt the *Spirit of Tasmania* was stolen by pirates.'

'You're going by *boat*?'

She shuffled in her seat. 'I thought you of all people would appreciate the adventure of my going by open sea.'

A muscle flickered in Bradley's cheek. Fair enough. A reclining seat on a luxury ferry wasn't exactly his brand of adventure. Sweat, pain, hard slog, the ultimate test of will and courage and fortitude, man proving himself worthy against unbeatable odds—that was his thing. She was secretly packing seasickness tablets.

Every time she'd been on a boat with him she picked the most central spot in which to sit, and tended to stare at the horizon a good deal of the time. Trying to keep her failing hidden in order to appear the perfect employee. Irreplaceable.

She was hardly going to tell him that the real reason she'd booked the day-long trip rather than a one-hour flight was that, while she was very much looking forward to the break, she was dreading going home. A twelve-hour boat trip was heaven-sent! She'd been back to Tassie once in the seven years since she'd left home. For her mother's fiftieth birthday extravaganza. Or so she'd been told. It had, in fact, been her mother's third wedding—to some schmuck who'd made a fortune in garden tools. She'd felt blindsided. Her mother hadn't understood why. Poor Elyse, then sixteen, had been caught in the middle. It had been an unmitigated disaster.

So, if she had to endure twelve hours of eating nothing but dry crackers and pinching the soft spot between her thumb and forefinger to fight off motion sickness, it would be worth it.

'Ever been to Tasmania?' she asked, glad to change the subject.

He shook his head. 'Can't say I have.'

Hannah sat forward on her seat, mouth agape. '*No*? That's a travesty! It's just over the pond, for goodness' sake! And it's gorgeous. Much of it is rugged and untouched. Just your cup of tea. The jagged cliffs of Queenstown, where it appears as though copper has been torn from the land by a giant's claws. Ocean Beach off Strahan, where the winds from the Roaring Forties tear across of the most unforgiving coastline. And then there's Cradle Mountain. That's where the wedding's being held. Cold and craggy and simply stunning, resting gorgeously and menacingly on the edge of the most beautiful crystal-clear lake. And that's just a tiny part of the west coast. The whole island is magical. So lush and raw and diverse and pretty and challenging...'

She stopped to take a breath, and glanced from the spot in mid-air she'd been staring through to find Bradley watching her. His deep grey eyes pinned her to her seat as he listened. *Really* listened. As though her opinion mattered *that* much.

Her heart began to pound like crazy. It was a heady thought. But dangerous all the same. The fact that he was unreachable, an island unto himself, was half the appeal of indulging in an impossible crush. It didn't cost her anything but the occasional sleepless night.

She stood quickly and slung her heavy leather satchel over her shoulder. 'And on that note...'

Bradley stood as well. A move born of instinct. It still felt nice.

Well, there were millions of men who would stand when she stood. Thousands at the very least. There was a chance one or two of them would even be at her sister's bigger-than-*Ben Hur* wedding. Maybe looking for a little romance. A little fun. Looking for someone with whom to unwind.

Maybe more…

She took two steps back. 'I hope New Zealand knocks your socks off.'

'Have a good weekend, Hannah. Don't do anything I wouldn't do.'

She shot him a quick smile. 'Have no fear. I have no intention of dropping off or picking up any dry-cleaning this weekend.'

He laughed, the unusually relaxed sound rumbling through her. She vibrated. Inside and out.

As Bradley curled back into his chair Hannah tugged her hair out from under the strap of her bag, slipped on her oversized sunglasses, took a deep breath of the crisp winter air, and headed for the tram stop that would take her to her tiny Fitzroy apartment.

And that was how Hannah's first holiday in nearly a year began. Her first trip home in three years. The first time she'd seen her mother face to face since she'd married. *Again.*

Let the panic begin…

CHAPTER TWO

HANNAH was in the bathroom, washing sleep out of her eyes, when her apartment doorbell rang just before six the next morning. It couldn't be the cab taking her to the dock; it wasn't due for another hour.

'Can you get that?' she called out, but no sound or movement came from Sonja's room.

Hannah ran her fingers through her still messy bed hair and rushed to the door.

She opened it to find herself looking at the very last view she would ever have expected. Bradley, in her favourite of his leather jackets—chocolate-brown and wool-lined—and dark jeans straining under the pressure of all that hard-earned muscle. Tall, gorgeous and wide awake, standing incongruously in the hallway outside her tiny apartment. It was so ridiculous she literally rubbed her eyes.

When she opened them he was still there, in all his glory—only now his eyes were roving slowly over her flannelette pyjama pants, her dad's over-sized, faded, thirty-year-old Melbourne University jumper, her tatty old Ugg boots.

Even while she fought the urge to hide behind the door, the feel of those dark eyes slowly grazing her body was beautifully illicit.

'Can I come in?' he asked, eyes sliding back to hers.

No *good morning*. No *sorry to bother you*. No *I've obviously arrived at a bad time*. Just right to the point.

'Now?' She glanced over her shoulder, glad Sonja's make-shift clothesline, usually laden with silky nothings and hanging from windowframe to windowframe, had been mysteriously taken down during the night.

'I have a proposal.'

He had a proposal? At six in the morning? That couldn't wait? What could she do but wave a welcoming arm?

He took two steps inside, and instantly the place felt smaller than it actually was. And it was already pretty small. Kitchenette, lounge, two beds, one bath. Small windows looking out over nothing much. Plenty for two working women who just needed a place to crash.

She closed the apartment door and leant against it as she waited for him to complete his recce.

Compared with his monstrous pad, with its multiple rooms and split-levels and city views, it must seem like a broom closet.

When he turned back to her, those grey eyes gleaming like molten silver in the early-morning light, the pads of her fingers pressed so hard into the panelled wood at her back her knuckles ached.

But he was all business. 'I hope you're almost ready. Flight's in two hours.'

She blinked. Suddenly as wide awake as if she was three coffees down rather than none. Had he forgotten? Again? She pushed away from the door and her hands flew to her hips. 'Are you kidding me?'

His cheek twitched. 'You can get that look off your face. I'm not here to throw you over my shoulder and whisk you off to New Zealand.'

She swallowed—half-glad, half-disappointed. 'You're not?'

'The ferry would take a full day to get to Launceston. I looked it up. It seems a ridiculous waste of time when I have a plane that could get you there in an hour. As such, I'm flying you to Tasmania.'

'What about New Zealand? It took me a month to organise the whole team to fly in from—'

'We're making a detour. Now, hurry up and get ready.'

'But—'

'You can thank me later.'

Thank him? The guy had just gone and nixed her brilliant plan to take a full twelve hours in which to rev herself up to facing her mother, while at the same time putting lots of lovely miles between herself and him. And he was doing so in what appeared to be an effort at being *nice*. If things continued along in the same vein as her day had so far, Sonja would walk out of her room and announce she was joining a nunnery.

'It's decided.' He took a step her way.

She held her hands out in front of her, keeping him at bay and keeping herself from jumping over the coffee table and throttling him. 'Not by me it's not.'

He was stubborn. But then so was she. Her dad had been a total sweetheart—a push-over even when it came to those he'd loved. Her occasional mulishness was the one trait she couldn't deny she'd inherited from her mum.

'I know how hard you work. And compared with most people I've come across in this industry, you do so with great grace and particularity. I appreciate it. So, please, hitch a ride on me.'

The guy was trying so hard to say thank-you, in his own roundabout way, he looked as if a blood vessel was about to burst in his forehead.

Hannah threw her hands in the air and growled at the gods before saying, 'Fine. Proposal accepted.'

He breathed out hard, and the tension eased from him until his natural energy level eased from eleven back to its usual nine and a half.

He nodded, then looked over his shoulder, decided only the couch would take his bulk, and moved past her to sit down. There he picked up a random magazine from the coffee table and pretended to be interested in the '101 Summer Hair Tips' it promised to reveal inside its pages.

'We leave in forty-five minutes.'

Well, it seemed happy, lovely, thank-you time was over. Back to business as usual.

Hannah glanced at her dad's old diving watch, which was so overly big for her she had to twist it to read it. Forty-five minutes? She'd be ready in forty.

Without another word she spun and raced into her room. She grabbed the comfy, Tasmania-in-winter-appropriate travel outfit she'd thrown over the tub chair in the corner the night before, and rushed into the bathroom.

Sonja was there, in a bottle-green Japanese silk kimono, plucking her eyebrows.

Hannah's boots screeched to a halt on the tiled floor. 'Sonja! Jeez, you scared me half to death. I didn't even know you were home.'

Sonja smiled into the mirror. 'Just giving you and the boss man some privacy.'

The smile was far too Cheshire-cat-like for comfort. Hannah suddenly remembered the unnaturally underwear-free window. 'You *knew* he was coming!'

Sonja threw her tweezers onto the sink and turned to Hannah. 'All I know is that from the moment we got back to the office yesterday arvo he was all about "Tasmania this, Tasmania that." Everything else was designated secondary priority.'

Hannah opened her mouth, but nothing came out.

Sonja pouted. 'He never offered to fly *me* home for the holidays, and I've been working for him for twice as long as you.'

'Your parents live a fifteen-minute tram-ride away.' Hannah

shoved her friend out, slamming the door with as much gusto as she could muster.

With time rushing through the hourglass, she whipped off her pyjamas and threw them into a pile on the closed lid of the toilet, then scrunched her hair into a knot atop her head as she didn't have time to do anything fancy with it, before standing naked beneath the cold morning spray of the tiny shower. Sucking in her stomach, she turned up the heat and waited till the temperature was just a little too hot for comfort before grabbing a cake of oatmeal soap and scrubbing away the languor of the night.

A plane ride, she thought. *Surrounded by camera guys, lighting guys, and Bradley's drier than toast accountant.* Then at the airport they'd go their separate ways, and she could get on with her holiday and remember what it felt like to live a life without Bradley Knight in the centre of it.

A little voice twittered in the back of her head. *If you'd taken either of the perfectly good jobs you've been offered in the past few months you'd know what that felt like on a permanent basis.*

Swearing with rather unladylike gusto, Hannah turned her back to the shower, letting the hot spray pelt her skin as she soaped random circles over her stomach. She let her forehead drop to thump against the cold glass.

Both jobs had sounded fine. Great, even. Leaps along the career path she sought. But working on studio-based programming just didn't hold the same excitement as travelling to places for which she needed a half-dozen shots. Trudging up mud slopes and down glaciers, canoeing rivers filled with crocodiles, even if she had to count back from a hundred so as not to heave over the side.

At some stage in the past year, small-town Hannah had become a big-time danger junkie. Professionally and personally. And it had everything to do with the man whose impossible work ethic had her feeling as if she was teetering between immense success and colossal failure in every given task.

It was crazy-making. *He* was crazy-making. He was a self-contained, hard to know, ball-breaker. But, oh, the thrill that came when together they got it right.

She shivered. Deliciously. From top to toe.

She just wasn't ready to let that go.

Suddenly she realised she had the shower up so high she was actually beginning to sweat. She could feel it tingling across her scalp, in the prickling of her palms. She licked her lips to find they tasted of salt.

She turned to lean her back against the cool of the door, only to find the water wasn't so hot after all. And she was still sliding the slick soap over her shoulders, down her arms, around her torso, in a slow, rhythmic movement as her head was filled with impenetrable smoky grey eyes, dark wavy hair, a roguish five o'clock shadow, shoulders broad enough to carry the weight of the world...

Heat pulsed in her centre, radiating outwards until she had to breathe through her mouth to gather enough oxygen to remain upright. She wrapped her arms tight around her.

Brilliant, beautiful, intense—and literally on the other side of the door. With no sound in the apartment bar the sound of the running shower. And the door was unlocked. Heck, the walls were so old and warped she had a floor mat shoved at the base of the door to keep it closed. With his bulk, if he walked too hard on the creaky floorboards the thing might spring open.

What if that happened and he looked up to find her naked, wet, slippery? Alone. Skin pink from the steaming hot spray. More so from thoughts of him.

What would he do? Would it finally occur to him that she was actually a woman, not just a walking appointment book?

No, it wouldn't. And thank God for that. For if he ever

looked at her in *that* way she wouldn't even know what to do. They worked together like a dream, but as for the paths they'd taken to stumble into one another? The man was so far removed from her reality he was practically a different species.

'Perfect, safe, fantasy material for a girl too busy to get her kicks any other way,' she told the wall.

But somehow it had sounded far more sophisticated in her head than it did out loud. Out loud it sounded as though the time was nigh for her to get a life.

She determinedly put the lathered soap on the tray and turned off the taps.

She then reached for her towel—only to find in her rush she'd left it hanging on a hook on the back of her bedroom door.

She glanced at the musty PJs piled on the lid of the toilet, and then at the minuscule handtowel hanging within reach. She let her head thunk back against the shower wall.

The pipes in the pre-war building creaked as the shower was turned off in Hannah's bathroom.

Finally. Bradley had told her they only had forty-five minutes, and the damn woman had been in the shower for what felt like for ever.

Bradley loosened his grip on the magazine he'd been clutching the entire time the shower had run—to find his fingers had begun to cramp.

'Coffee?' Sonja said, swanning out from nowhere.

He'd been so sure they were alone—just him in the lounge, Hannah in the shower, nothing but twelve feet of open space and a thin wooden door between them—he jumped halfway out of his skin.

'Where the hell did you spring from?' he growled.

'Around,' Sonja said, waving a hand over her shoulder as she swept towards a gleaming espresso machine that took up half the tiny kitchen bench. It was the only thing that looked as if it had had any real money spent on it in the whole place.

The rest was fluffy faded rugs, pink floral wallpaper, and tasselled lampshades so ancient-looking every time his eyes landed on one he felt he needed to sneeze. He felt as if he was sitting in the foyer of an old-time Western brothel, waiting for the madam to put in an appearance.

Not what he would have expected of Hannah's pad—if he'd ever thought of it at all.

She was hard-working. Meticulous. With a reserve of stamina hidden somewhere in her small frame that meant she was able to keep up with his frenetic pace where others had fallen away long before.

What she *wasn't* was abandoned, pink…frou-frou.

Or so he'd thought.

'I'm making one for myself so it's no bother.'

Bradley blinked to find he was staring so hard at Hannah's bathroom door it might have appeared as though he was hoping for a moment of X-ray vision. He threw the magazine on the table with enough effort to send it sliding onto the floor, then turned bodily away from the door to glance at Sonja.

'Coffee?' Sonja repeated, dangling a gaudy pink and gold espresso mug from the tip of her pink-taloned pinky.

It hit him belatedly that the apartment was pure Sonja. Of *course*. He vaguely remembered her telling him Hannah had at some stage that year moved in with her.

For some reason it eased his mind. The trust he had in Hannah's common sense hadn't been misplaced.

He glanced at his watch and frowned. Though if she didn't get a hurry on he was ready to revise that thought.

'A quick one,' he said.

Coffees made, Sonja perched on the edge of the pink-striped dining chair that sat where a lounge chair ought. 'So, you're schlepping our girl to the wilds of Tasmania?'

'On my way to the New Zealand recce.'

'Several hundred miles out of your way.'

'What's your point?'

'It's not my job to have a point. You pay me to build mystery and excitement,' she said, grinning. 'And what's more exciting and mystifying than you and Hannah heading off to have a wild time in the wild?'

'A wild—?' This time his frown was for real. He sat up as best he could in the over-soft old chair, and pointed two fingers in the direction of Sonja's nose. 'She works damned hard. I'm saying thanks. So don't you start cooking up any mad stories in that head of yours. You know how I don't like drama.'

Sonja stared right back, and then, obviously realising he was deadly serious, nodded and said, 'Whatever you say, boss.'

And with that she got up and strode back towards what must have been her bedroom.

'So long as you promise I'm the first one you'll tell when you have something else to say. About New Zealand,' she added, as an apparent afterthought.

And with a dramatic swish of silk she was gone.

Bradley sank slowly back into the soft couch and downed the hot espresso in one hit, letting it scorch the back of his throat.

If the woman wasn't so good at her job...

But he hadn't been kidding. He abhorred gratuitous drama. He'd gone miles out of his way to avoid it his whole life. Up remote mountains, down far-flung rivers in the middle of nowhere, deep into uninhabited jungles. Dedicating his life to concrete pleasures. Real challenges he could see and touch. Facing the raw and unbroken parts of the world in order to discover what kind of man he *really* was, rather than the kind life had labelled him the moment he was born.

Far, far away from the histrionics he'd endured as a kid, both before and after his hypersensitive mother had decided that being *his* mother was simply too hard. Leaving him to the mercy of whichever relative had had the grace to take him that month and increasing the drama tenfold. Every one of them had expected him to be volubly and effusively grateful they'd taken on such an encumbrance as he. The telling of it had become a daily litany. But that had been nothing compared with the horrendously uncomfortable drama that rocked each household the moment the inhabitants realised that they were not, in fact, as altruistic as they'd imagined they were.

Then they'd each and every one whispered behind half-closed doors, perhaps it wasn't *their* fault. His own mother had given him away after all...

A flash of something appeared out of the corner of Bradley's eye, slapping him back to the absolute present. He sat forward, leant his elbows on his knees, and ran his hands hard and fast over his face in an effort to rub the prickly remnants of memory away.

Then all thought fled his mind as he realised what the flash had been. Hannah. Dashing from the bathroom into her bedroom. Naked.

He slowly turned his head to look at the empty spot where the vision had appeared. Piece by piece it slipped into his mind.

A wet female back, a pair of lean wet legs, and a small white handtowel covering nought but what must have been wet naked buttocks.

Hannah. *Naked.* And right at that moment behind that door, towelling down with something about the size of a postage stamp.

From nowhere a swift, steady heat began to surface inside him. An unmistakable heat. The kind he'd usually invite with open arms.

He dragged his eyes back to the front and stared hard at a pink quilted lamp covered in so many tassels it made his eyes hurt. Better that than focus on the image seemingly burned into the backs of his eyes.

Hannah was hard-working, meticulous, with a reserve of stamina… He stopped when he realised he was repeating himself *to* himself.

A loud bang came from Hannah's room, after which rang out a badly muffled oath and what sounded like hopping.

He found himself coughing out a laugh. Relief flooded through him, and the unfortunate heat brimming inside him dissipated, somewhat. *That* was the Hannah he knew. Hard-working, meticulous, and singularly likely to snap him out of the labyrinth of his mind right when he needed it most.

At that moment Hannah came bounding out of her room. Fully dressed. In fact she appeared to be wearing a grey blanket as she dragged a big black suitcase behind her.

He managed to pull himself from the clutches of the soft couch to stand, just as she plonked her suitcase by the door and turned to face him. Lips parted, breathless. From the suitcase? The hopping? The exertion of running to her room wet and naked?

He gave himself a mental slap.

'You made yourself coffee?' she said, staring at the coffee table.

'Sonja.'

'Oh. *Oh!*' Her eyes opened unnaturally wide, then flicked to the room into which Sonja had disappeared. 'Did she…? Did you…?'

He raised an eyebrow.

But she just shook her head, a new pinkness staining her cheeks and a telling kind of darkness in her eyes. It was the kind of look that told a specific story without need for words. It was the kind of look, when added to the image of naked female flesh, that could turn a man's blood to hot oil.

Though it was far more likely he simply hadn't fully moved on from the 'flash' after all.

You're a man, he growled to himself, *not a rock. Don't be so hard on yourself.*

Suddenly Hannah held up a finger and headed over to the small round table behind the couch, flicked through a bunch of papers. Ignoring him completely. He gave his head a short, sharp shake.

As she moved, Hannah's voluminous blanket—which turned out to be some kind of poncho—shifted, revealing that in lieu of her usual filmy, elegant work number she wore dark skinny jeans tucked into cowboy boots, and a fitted black and red striped, long-sleeved top. Truly fitted. Giving him glimpses of the kind of gentle curves that her filmy, floaty, elegant work numbers had clearly never made the most of.

Curves he'd glimpsed naked, with no embellishment. Curves he could almost feel beneath his hands.

Gritting his teeth, Bradley leant his backside against the edge of the couch and waited. And watched. With the early-morning sun streaming through the old window behind her she looked so young, so fresh. Her nose was pink in the morning cold, her cheeks even pinker. Her lips were naturally the colour of a dark rose. She had a smattering of freckles across her nose he'd never before noticed. And her usually neat, professional hair was kinky and shaggy, as if she'd come from a day at the beach. As if she'd just rolled out of bed.

She glanced up to find him staring. After a beat she smiled in apology. 'Two seconds. I promise.'

He cleared his throat. 'If I didn't know better I'd think you were purposely delaying getting moving.'

She blinked at him, several times, super-fast. Then shook her head so quickly he wondered if his sorry excuse for a joke had actually hit its mark. But he knew so little about her outside of how well she did her job he couldn't be sure.

'Sonja is clueless about paying bills,' she went on. 'It's too cold a winter for me to risk her getting the heating cut off—

even though I can think of a dozen reasons why she might deserve it.'

He found himself stepping over a line he didn't usually breach as he asked, 'Why do I get the feeling there's some other reason you're avoiding heading out that door?'

'I—' She swallowed. Then looked him dead in the eye for several long seconds before offering a slight shrug and saying, 'It's not that I don't want to go back home. I love that island more than anything. I'm just bracing myself for what I am about to encounter when I step across the Gatehouse threshold.'

'The Gatehouse?'

'The hotel.'

'Regretting your choice?'

That earned him a glance from pale green eyes that could cut glass. 'You truly think I would organise for my only sister to get married in some *dive*?'

'I guess it depends if you like your only sister. How long did you say it's been since you've seen her?'

Her cheeks turned pinker still: a bright, warm, enchanting pink as blood rushed to her face. But she chose to ignore his insinuation. 'The Gatehouse, I'll have you know, is a slice of pure heaven. Like a Swiss chalet, tucked into a forest of snow-dappled gumtrees. A mere short hike to the stunning Cradle Mountain. A hundred beautiful rooms, six gloriously decadent restaurants, a fabulous nightclub, a cinema, a state-of-the-art gym. And don't even get me started on the suites.'

Her eyes drifted shut and she shuddered. No, it was more like a tremble. It started at her shoulders and shimmied down her form, finishing up at her boot-clad feet, one of which had lifted to tuck in tight behind her opposite calf.

Sensation prickled down his arms, across his abdomen, between his thighs. He could do nothing but stand there, grit his teeth, and hope to high heaven she'd soon be done and he could get away from this crazy pink boudoir before it fried any more of his brain cells.

Hell. Who was this woman, and where had she put his trusty assistant?

If it were not for those wide, wide, frank pale green eyes that looked right into his, not the tiniest bit intimidated by his infamy, bull-headedness or insularity, he'd be wondering if he was in the right apartment.

That would teach him to try and do something nice for somebody else. Another lesson learnt.

Her foot slid down her calf, and as though nothing had happened she went back to the pile of papers.

'Okay,' she said. 'I think we can safely assume Sonja will survive till Tuesday.' She ruffled a hand through her hair, and it ended up looking even more loose and carefree and sexy as hell. 'I'm ready.'

She ruffled a hand through her hair, and it ended up looking even more loose and carefree, and sexy as hell.

His hands grew restless, as if he wasn't quite sure where to put them. As if they wanted to go somewhere his brain knew they ought not.

So he gave them a job and grabbed the handle of her suitcase. One yank and his stomach muscles clenched. 'What did you pack in here? Bricks?'

A hand slunk to her hip, buried somewhere deep beneath acres of grey wool, temptingly hiding more than they revealed.

'Yes,' she said. 'I have filled the bag with bricks—not, as one might assume, a long weekend's worth of clothes, shoes and underthings that will take me from day to night, PJs to wedding formal. Have you never been to a wedding before?'

'Never.'

'Wow. I'm not sure if you've missed out or if you're truly the luckiest man alive. While you're trekking through some of the most beautiful scenery in the world—bar Tasmania's, of course—I'll be changing outfits more times than a pop singer in a film clip.'

Bradley closed his eyes to stop the vision *that* throwaway comment brought forth before it could fully manifest itself inside his head.

'Car's downstairs,' he growled, hefting the bag out through her front door. 'Be there in five minutes or your—'

Underthings that will take you from day to night.

'Your gear and I will be gone without you.'

'Okey-dokey.'

With a dismissive wave over her shoulder she went looking for Sonja to say her goodbyes.

Feeling oddly as if a small pair of hands had just unclenched themselves from the front of his shirt, Bradley was out of that door and away from all that soft velvet, stifling frills and frou-frou pink that had clearly been chosen specifically in order to scramble a man's brains.

To the airport, up in the plane, drop her off, thanks gifted—and then to New Zealand he and his research crew would go. He, his research crew, and a juvenile intern who could spend half the day discussing 'underthings' and not affect his blood pressure in the slightest.

CHAPTER THREE

HANNAH stood in the doorway of the Gulfstream jet.

Place? Launceston, Tasmania.

Time of arrival? Mid-morning.

Temperature? Freezing.

She breathed in the crisp wintry air though her nose. Boy, did it smell amazing. Soft, green, untainted. She could actually hear birds singing. And the sky was so clear and blue it hurt her eyes. A small smile crept into the corners of her mouth.

She hadn't been sure how she'd feel, stepping foot back on Tassie soil after such a long time in Melbourne. How parochial the place would feel in comparison with her bustling cosmopolitan base.

It felt like home.

A deep voice behind her said, 'What? No "welcome home" banner? No marching band?'

'Oh, Lord,' she said as she jumped. Then, 'I'm going, I'm going! You can get on your way. Go back inside. It's freezing.'

'I'm a big boy. I can handle the cold.' Bradley threw the last of a bag of macadamia nuts into his mouth as he looked over her shoulder. 'So this is Tasmania.'

She looked out over Launceston International Airport. One simple flat-roofed building sat on the edge of acres of pocked grey Tarmac. A light drizzle thickened the cold air. Patches of old snow lay scattered in pockets of shade, while the rest of the ground was covered in little melted puddles.

As far as first impressions went it was hardly going to ring Bradley's adventure-savvy bell.

'No,' she said, 'this is an airport. Tasmania is the hidden wonder beyond.'

'Get a move on, then. I don't have all day.'

She shook her head. 'Sorry. Of course. Thanks. For the lift. But, please, I don't need one back. I'll see you Tuesday.'

With that she gave him a short wave, before jogging down the stairs—only to see the pilot had her bags plonked on the Tarmac next to another set of luggage that looked distinctly like Bradley's.

'What's he doing?' she asked. Then turned to find Bradley was right behind her.

Instinct had her slamming her hands against his chest so as not to topple onto her backside. Her hips against his thighs. Her right knee wedged hard between his.

Hard muscles clenched instantly beneath her touch. Hot, hard, Bradley-shaped muscles.

All she could think was that, God, he felt good. Big. Strong. Solid. Warm. All too real. She blinked up into his eyes to find glinting circles of deepest grey staring down at her.

'You're shaking,' he said, glowering as though she had somehow offended his sensibilities.

She curled her fingers into her palms and hid them beneath her poncho as she took a distinct step back, her body arching towards him even while she dragged herself away. 'Of course I'm shaking. It's barely above zero.'

He looked out across the Tarmac, as though for a moment he'd forgotten where they were. Then his hand hovered to where her hands had been against his chest. He scratched the spot absent-mindedly. 'Really?' he rumbled. 'I hadn't noticed.'

Truth was, neither had she. For, while the wind-chill factor had probably taken the temperature *below* zero, she was still feeling a tad feverish after being bodily against a human furnace.

Hannah took another step back. 'Why has James deposited your luggage beside mine?'

'I'm researching.'

'What? The difference between Tarmac in Tasmanian and New Zealand airports?'

Humour flickered behind his eyes. It made her senses skedaddle and a purely feminine heat began to pulse. Then he slid his sunglasses into their usual hiding place and she had no chance of reading him.

'Less specific,' he said dryly. 'Try Tasmania.' Then he sauntered on past.

'Wait!' she called. 'Hang on just a minute. What am I missing here?'

'You sell yourself short on your PR abilities. You sold me.'

'Sold you what?'

'Tracts of wild, rugged, untouched beauty. Jagged cliffs. Lush forests. Roaring waterfalls. Lakes so still you don't know which way is the sky. Sound familiar?'

Sure did. One of her many effusive speeches about her gorgeous home.

He continued, 'It got me to thinking. So it's decided. The team know what to do in New Zealand. They'll go that way, while I do a solo recce of this area this weekend.'

So that was what they'd been cooking up in the back of the jet. She'd been busy playing holiday, so as not to get caught up in office stuff—sipping on a cocktail, reading a trashy magazine and listening to the music blaring from her iPod—and she'd blissfully let it all go by.

She must have been gaping like a beached fish, because he added, 'Don't panic. I have no intention of invading your holiday. Spencer's hired me a car and planned me a course.'

Hannah snapped her mouth shut. The fact that he was staying was still beyond her comprehension. But mostly she was struggling with the intense sense of envy that the one time she'd cut herself off was the one time she could have proved her producer potential. Sure, Spencer was great with an online map, but *nobody* in Bradley's circle knew the island, the detail, the most TV-worthy spots of her home island more than her.

Her timing couldn't have sucked more.

An insistent voice knocked hard on the back of her brain. *Let it go. Give yourself a muuuuuch needed break. And come Tuesday sit him down and tell him exactly why he needs to put you in charge of the project.*

'Okay,' she said, overly bright. 'Well, that's just…excellent. Truly. You won't regret it.'

With that she turned away and headed towards her luggage. And that was when she heard it. A penetrating feminine voice shrilled thinly in the far distance.

'Yoo-hoo! Hannah! Over *heeeeere*!'

Her conflicted emotions fled in an instant at the sound of that voice. And, boy, did she not blame them?

Why? How?

The text! She'd sent Elyse a quick message saying she'd be getting in early, and how. Dammit!

'Hannah!'

She frantically searched the small crowd awaiting the arrival of loved ones from behind a chicken wire fence. With their matching long, thick and straight dark brown hair, pale skin, shiny baubles, and head to toe pink get-ups, Hannah's mother and sister stood out from the small, chilly, rugged-up crowd like flamingos in a flock of pigeons.

As though the years hadn't passed—as though she didn't have an amazing job and a great apartment, cool friends and real confidence in where she'd landed—Hannah's hand went straight to her hair. Only to remember she'd done nothing with it that morning and now, as she stood on the windy Tarmac, it was making a fly for freedom in just about every direction possible.

In about five seconds flat she went from respected ace assistant to a TV wunderkind to skinny tomboy shuffling a soccer ball around the backyard while her glamorous mother and sister shopped and groomed and giggled about boys.

Her mother pushed through the crowd, opened a gate that probably meant she was breaking about half a dozen aviation safety laws, and headed her way. Hannah knew the grown-up thing to do was walk towards her, waving happily, but she was so deep into meltdown mode she began to physically back away.

And that was when she felt an arm slide beneath her poncho to settle gently but firmly in the curve of her back. The wall of warmth that came with it stopped her in her retreat as nothing else could have.

She must have been putting out such a silent distress call even her famously self-contained boss had felt it. Had come to her defence. Gallantry was becoming a bit of a pattern, in fact. If only the feel of him so close didn't also make her knees forget how to keep her legs straight.

And she needed every ounce of strength she had for what was about to happen. For coming up against her mother unprepared and un-liquored-up. And for subjecting her fuss-phobic boss to the living soap opera that was her family.

Bradley and her mother. Oh, no.

Brain suddenly working as if she had a sixth-sense, Hannah leaned in closer and said, 'Take a sharp left now, head into those bushes to the east and you'll hit the main road in about three minutes. Hail a cab from there. *Go!*'

His eyebrows came together and he laughed softly. 'Why on earth would I want to do that?'

'See that vision in pink hurtling our way? That's my mother.

And if you don't run now you'll feel like you've been hit by a hurricane.'

But it was too late.

She felt Bradley stiffen behind her. His fingers dug into her skin. If her brain hadn't been working overtime on how to keep her boss from going into a meltdown right alongside her she might just have groaned with the intense pleasure of it.

Virginia's eyes had zeroed in on Bradley with a vengeance. No wonder. A six-feet-four hunk standing in the shadow of his own private jet wasn't something any woman could easily ignore. Especially a strikingly beautiful woman currently between rich husbands.

Elyse, ever the mini-Mum, tottered in her wake.

Hannah felt Bradley grow an inch behind her as he breathed in deep. Then he broke the tense silence with, 'So, to downgrade the hurricane to mild sun shower, what do I need to know?'

Just like that, the Tarmac beneath her feet felt like familiar ground. At Knight Productions they never went into any meeting without being completely prepared for any outcome. Without knowing they'd never accept no for an answer. And Bradley always got his own way.

'Number one: call her Virginia,' Hannah punched out. 'Not *Mrs* anything. She's never liked to be thought of as a wife or mother. If people think she is either, it's proof she's of a certain age. Do that and you're ahead of the curve.'

Bradley's eyebrows all but disappeared into his hairline, but at least his death grip relaxed. 'Who does she think people think *you* were? Her fan club?'

Hannah laughed. Unexpectedly. She turned to find he was looking far more relaxed and less rock-like than she could ever have hoped. And as she turned his hand slipped further around her waist. Her breath went AWOL.

'Relax,' he murmured, leaning closer. 'You are so wound

up you're actually beginning to scare me just a little. Don't panic. Mothers love me.'

She shot him a look of despair. '*That's* not the problem. I mean, look at you. I have no doubt my mother will adore you.'

A muscle twitched beneath his eye and his mouth lifted into a sexy half-smile. 'You think I'm adorable?'

'To the tips of your designer socks,' she said, her voice as blank as she could manage. 'And, just for the record, along with *tall* men who *own* private jets my mother also adores rhinestones, tight pink cardigans and fruity cocktails with little umbrellas in them.'

The second the words were out of her mouth she regretted them. But it wasn't as though she never ribbed the guy. Working sixty-hour weeks a girl had to have a sense of humour. And he was oak-like enough to take it.

But comparing him with rhinestones…?

Maybe it was the comfy outfit. Maybe it was giving her brain cells a day off from the blow-dryer. Or maybe her body had gone into some kind of holiday-mode shutdown. Either way, her tongue had come dangerously loose.

So dangerously Bradley's hand slid even further—till it rested possessively on her hip, till his little finger slid between T-shirt and jeans and found skin. A silent signal that if she went one step too far she was at his mercy. As a comeback it was effective. Debilitatingly so.

Hannah was so tense she was practically vibrating.

She didn't have time to think before Virginia was upon them, long hair swinging like a shampoo commercial, high heels clacking loudly on the asphalt.

Then her mother's eyes zeroed in on the lack of sunlight between the two of them. Hannah wished she was wearing work stilettos so she could have kicked her boss in the shin.

'Hannah! Darling!' Virginia's eyes were gleaming, her arms outstretched, and she was looking Bradley up and down as though he was a two-hundred-dollar Hobart Bay lobster even while she reached out for the daughter she hadn't seen for three years.

Virginia's arm wrapped around her none too gently just as Bradley's hand slipped away. She gave in to one while missing the other.

'Virginia,' Hannah said. 'It's so nice of you to meet me, but you really shouldn't have. This weekend of all weekends.'

Over her mother's shoulder Hannah saw Elyse hovering. Her chest pinched at the happy tears in her little sister's bright green eyes.

She mouthed, *Hi*. Elyse did the same.

And then, in her ear, Hannah heard, 'He's very handsome.'

Not even a whisper. An out-and-out declaration. Heck, even James the pilot, who was now taxiing Bradley's jet down a nearby runway, had probably heard.

'He's my boss,' Hannah blurted, just as loud. 'Thus out of bounds. So leave him alone.'

Elyse hid a shocked laugh behind a fake sneeze.

Her mum pulled back and looked deep into her eyes with what looked like a flicker of respect. Wow. That was a first. Hannah's chest squeezed as she waited for…more. Sadness, poignancy, guilt, regret…

Until Virginia took a step back, flounced a hand up and down Hannah's form and said, 'Jeans, Hannah? Must you always look like a bag lady?'

And there you have it, folks. My mother.

'My work means I fly a lot. All over the world, in fact. I've learnt it pays to be comfortable.' She mentally blew a raspberry, not much caring that it made her feel five years old.

Having said all she apparently felt the need to say, Virginia slid her eyes back to Bradley. In his jeans and fitted shirt, and the soft old leather jacket, he looked extremely comfortable. He also looked good enough to eat.

The scent of macadamia emanating from his direction only made that thought solidify. And expand. Hannah had to swallow down the sensation that rocked through her, finishing in a slow burn shaped very much like a large hand-print upon her back.

'It seems my daughter hasn't the manners to introduce us…'

'Forgive me,' Hannah leapt in. 'Virginia, this is Bradley Knight—my boss. Bradley, this is Virginia Millar Gillespie McClure. My mother.'

Virginia's smile was saccharine-sweet, her eyes cool as she said, 'Darling, you forgot the Smythe. Though Derek *was* rather forgettable, I'm afraid.'

Bradley took off his sunglasses and hooked them over the neckline of his T-shirt before grasping the manicured hand coming at him at pace. Hannah held her breath. Rock was about to meet hurricane. She squinted in preparation for being in the line of fire of flying debris.

'A pleasure to meet you, Virginia,' Bradley said, his deep, sexy voice as smooth as silk. 'And, considering the fact that I've never seen anyone with quite the same stunning colour eyes as Hannah's, this must be Elyse.'

Virginia blinked her own dark brown eyes slowly as she uncurled her hand away from Bradley's and made room for him to pass her by in favour of her daughter. Not used to being upstaged, she stood there a moment in silence, regathering herself.

Hannah placed a hand over her mouth to cover her grin. If she hadn't had a soft spot for her boss before, she had one now.

Elyse's pale green eyes—eyes so much like their dad's—all but popped out of her head as she gravitated towards Bradley. 'Boy, it's an honour to meet you, Mr Knight. I love your shows.

So much. Adore them. Not just because Hannah works on them. They're actually really good too!'

Bradley laughed. 'Thank you. I think.'

Hannah slid the thumb of her right hand between her teeth and nibbled. Amazing. For a guy who usually turned to stone at the first sign of such dramatic declarations of adoration he was handling himself mighty well. She watched him carefully for signs that he was about to cut and run. But his smile seemed genuine.

Bradley's smiling gaze slowly swung to Hannah. His eyes widened just a fraction, enough to let her know that he was well aware he'd stepped into a little bit of crazy but was content to stay a while.

And the only reason she could think of for him to do such a thing was because of her. He'd known her trip home was short, and important, so he'd stepped up to the mark and helped her get there sooner. He'd realised that reuniting with her mother was not quite so looked forward to. So he'd moved in to protect her.

The ground at her feet suddenly felt less like Tarmac and more like jelly.

And then she realised that Elyse was still talking.

'Hannah never mentioned she was bringing a plus one, but of course we'll make room—right, Virginia? Hannah's so secretive about her life in Melbourne—the yummy celebrities she meets at all those TV parties and the guys she's dating. We can get all the goss from you instead!'

'No, no, *no*,' Hannah leapt in. 'Elyse, Bradley's not here to—'

'You *are* coming to the wedding,' Virginia insisted, stepping smack-bang between Hannah and her boss. 'The accommodation is six-star. The food to die for. Cradle Mountain is the most beautiful spot on the entire planet. Bar none. You simply cannot come to Tasmania without experiencing her raw beauty for yourself. In fact it's just the kind of place you should set one of your little shows.'

Hannah shook her head so hard she whipped herself in the eye with a hunk of hair. She slid into the fray and grabbed Bradley by the elbow, practically heaving him out of the clutches of her wily relations. 'Bradley's not here for the wedding. He's here on business. He doesn't even have a minute to spare and stand around here nattering. Do you, Bradley?'

'I couldn't possibly impose so last-minute,' was his response.

She glared up into his eyes to find he was refusing to look at her. Then he shifted his stance, so that her hand slid into the all too comfortable crook of his elbow. Heat slid slyly down her arm.

She tried to pull away. He only clamped down tighter. Then he smiled at her, a quicksilver gleam in his deep, smoky grey eyes.

Her heart tumbled in her chest and she slipped her hand free. Oh, God. Oh, no.

She should *never* have compared him with rhinestones, or tight pink cardigans, or fruity cocktails with little umbrellas in them. He wasn't protecting her. He was punishing her!

'Don't be ridiculous,' Virginia said, linking her hand through his spare elbow. 'Great-Aunt Maude left word last night to say she's entirely sure she's come down with consumption.'

Elyse rolled her eyes. 'For the engagement party it was malaria. Apart from the hypochondria she's the perfect great-aunt. She sends gifts ahead of time!'

Virginia turned towards the terminal and tugged Bradley in her wake. Hannah, as always, had no choice but to follow.

Virginia was saying, 'So there's a spare meal already paid for.'

Elyse, who had taken Bradley's now free other elbow, said, 'And the gift's taken care of too! We'll just pencil your name alongside Great-Aunt Maude's on the card. She'll never know. You won't be sitting with Hannah, as she'll be with Roger all night. But you seem like a man who can take care of himself.'

Hannah rolled her eyes. When they settled back into their normal position she realised Bradley was frowning at her.

'Roger?' he asked, his tone strangely accusing.

'The best man,' Elyse explained. 'He's a fitness guru. As maid of honour she'll be stuck to the guy like glue for the duration. But we'll find you a fun table, I promise.'

'Besides,' Virginia said, 'you're the reason our girl hasn't been able to drag herself away till now. You owe us, so we won't take no for an answer. Now, I'll go find some people to do something about your luggage and get you a hire car. Ours is filled to the brim with things for the wedding, otherwise I'd happily ride shotgun while you took my wheel.' She patted him on the cheek before bustling ahead, with Elyse at her heels.

Bradley slowed up till Hannah was beside him.

'I told you to run,' she said.

'Yes, you did.' He shook his head in wonder, then his cheek kicked into a half-smile that had her heart galloping all over again.

'You can't come,' Hannah said.

He was silent for a beat. Two. She was sure he was about to agree wholeheartedly—until he looked down at her and said, 'And why not?'

With his eyes on her, she said, 'Because you'd cramp my style.'

The sun was behind him, so she couldn't see his eyes, but the rumble in his voice more than made up for it. 'Would I, now?'

She felt a smile creep across her face, and her impish streak flashed back to life as her mother disappeared from view. 'You'll never know.'

His, 'Mmmm…' was far too non-committal for comfort. 'So, how does your father cope around all that frenetic feminine energy?'

Hannah's smile faded. She fiddled with her father's old watch. 'He died when I was fourteen.'

And from the moment it had happened she'd felt like Cinderella, left all alone with the step-family—only the family she'd been left with was her own.

She felt Bradley's eyes on her as she explained. 'He adored Virginia to bits. Elyse and I actually thought it rather disgusting how often we caught them kissing at the kitchen sink. Then he died. And she remarried within six months. Things have been particularly cool between us ever since.'

Several moments passed before Bradley said, 'I'm sorry to hear that.'

'Thanks.'

In the quiet of the great open space, Hannah wondered if the time was right, for the first time, to ask about *his* family. She had no idea if his parents were alive or dead. Missionaries or UFO-chasers. Or the King and Queen of some small European country populated by only the most beautiful people. Or if he spent Sunday lunch with them every weekend.

But at the last second she baulked, unsure how far to press the quiet moment. Instead she just said, 'Mum's been married again. Twice to date.'

Promising to love and honour each of them with as much supposed vim as she had their lovely father. Each and every time clearly nothing more than a pretty lie. It was why Hannah would never make another person such a promise unless she really meant it. Unless she knew she would be assured of the same level of commitment right back. The idea of doing anything else made her feel physically ill.

She looked to where her mother was now drumming up help in the shape of goodness knew who.

She felt Bradley turn away to watch Virginia. Moth to a flame. Then he said, 'Your mother…'

Hannah stiffened, preparing for the thing she'd heard a million times before. *Your mum's so glamorous. And Elyse is like a little doll. While you are…different.*

'She's…' Bradley paused again. 'I do believe that dress of hers is the place ruffles come to die.'

Hannah laughed so unexpectedly, so effusively, so delightedly, it fast turned into a cough.

Bradley gave her a thump on the back. It only made her cough all the harder. And feel *absolutely* certain that her earlier fantasies of Bradley doing anything out of a deeply buried sense of human-being-like protection were just that. Fantasies. The likes of which she needed this long weekend without him in order to stamp out.

Once she'd caught her breath, she said, 'Virginia does like her ruffles. As well as her pink fluffy cardigans and cocktails with umbrellas in them.'

The rhinestones went without saying, but the crease in his cheek told her he'd heard her all the same.

She smiled. She couldn't help herself.

Then, as though he too felt the strange familiarity building between then, he frowned and looked away, up at the clear crisp sky. He sniffed in a trail of ice-cold air and thrust his hands into his pockets. Shutting her out.

And there she was, feeling like a satellite to his moon. If that wasn't reason enough to put an end to her impossible crush, she didn't know what was.

'The day is moving on and we're standing still. Time to get a move on. I'll drop you at your resort and then be on my way.'

'*Resort?*' Hannah could all but hear her exclamation bouncing off the band of clouds hovering above the hills in the distance.

Bradley didn't even flinch. 'Spencer's itinerary has me

starting at Cradle Mountain. I studied his route, and it actually makes good sense. As does giving you a lift, since you clearly need one.'

Hannah snapped her mouth shut. If she'd been in charge of setting his itinerary she would have said the same. But she was on holiday. Out of the loop. And, yes, she *was* in need of a ride.

She threw her hands in the air and headed for the terminal.

He followed, his long legs catching up with her in two short strides.

She swallowed down the lick of envy at the happy tone in his voice. 'This car that Spencer hired had better be something big and solid. The roads on this island can get mighty windy.'

'It's a black roadster. Soft-top.' His large hands waved slowly through the air, as though he was tracing its curves in his mind.

Never before had Hannah felt so jealous of a machine.

'Are you kidding me? Seems to me he's passed on his drooling habits.'

A gentle kind of laughter tickled her ears.

She walked faster. But with his long, strong legs the blackguard kept up without any effort at all.

CHAPTER FOUR

'ARE we there yet?' Hannah muttered, stretching as much of herself as she could in the confined space of the ridiculous sports car Spencer had blithely allowed their valuable boss to zoom around in. She'd be having a talk with him when they got home!

'Turn left in eight hundred metres,' said the deep Australian drawl of the GPS.

'Ken,' she said, 'you are, as ever, my hero.'

'Who on earth is Ken?' Bradley asked, uttering his first words in nearly two hours. His mind was undoubtedly focussed on the embarrassment of gorgeous scenery they'd passed from Launceston to the mountain.

'Ken's the GPS guy.'

'You've *named* him?' he asked.

'His mother named him. I just chose his voice when you were busy pretending to check the car for prior damage while actually drooling over the chassis. I'm certain you would have preferred Swedish Una, or British Catherine, but it seemed only fair that, since you and my mother have railroaded me over and over again today, I got my way about one tiny part of my holiday.'

'Your way is *Ken*?'

'Don't you use that tone when you talk about Ken. I'll have you know I have him to thank for getting me out of many an oncoming tram disaster when I first moved to Melbourne.'

He glanced her way, giving her nothing more than a glimpse of her reflection in his sunglasses. 'So your idea of the perfect man is one with a good sense of direction?'

'I have no idea what my idea of the perfect man is. I've yet to meet one who even came close.'

She watched Bradley from the corner of her eye, waiting for his reaction to her jibe. He just lifted his hand from the windowsill and ran it across his mouth.

She fluffed her poncho till it settled like a blanket across her knees and said, 'Though Ken *is* reliable. And smart. And always available. And he cares about what I want.'

'Turn left. Then you have reached your destination,' Ken said, proving himself yet again.

Before she even felt the words coming Hannah added, 'And, boy, does he have the sexiest voice on the planet.'

Bradley's hand stopped short. Mid-chin-stroke. It slowly lowered to the steering wheel. 'And there I was thinking he sounds a bit like me.'

He moved the car down a gear. Slowed. Then turned from the road onto a long, gumtree-lined drive. Hannah stared demurely ahead and said, 'Nah.'

But the truth was that Ken's deep, sexy Australian drawl reminded her so much of Bradley's she'd often found herself turning her GPS on even when driving home on the rainy days she drove her little car to work rather than take a tram. She'd told herself it was the comfort of feeling as if there was someone else in the car when driving dark streets at night.

She'd lied.

And then, appearing from between a mass of grey-green flora sprinkled in glittering melting white snow, there was the Gatehouse. A grand façade dotted with hundreds of windows, dozens of chimneys and fantasy turrets. It was like something out of a fairytale, rising magnificent and fantastical out of the Australian scrub.

'If this is the Gatehouse,' Bradley said, slowing to a stop

so that the sports car rumbled throatily beneath them, 'what's behind the gate?'

Hannah placed a hand on his arm, doing her best to ignore the frisson scooting through her at even the simplest of contacts, and pointed to their left. Between two turrets there was a glimpse of the reason a chalet-style hotel could exist in such a remote place.

The stunning, stark, ragged peaks of Cradle Mountain.

Bradley slid his glasses from his face, eyebrows practically disappearing beneath his hairline. 'God must be a cinematographer at heart to dream up this place.'

'I know!' Hannah said, practically bouncing on her seat. When she realised she was tugging at his sleeve, she let go and sat back and contained herself.

Bradley's eyes slid to the building towering over them. 'How many rooms?'

'Enough for cast and crew.'

He finally dragged his eyes from the picture-perfect view to look at her. They were gleaming with the thrill of the find. The buzz of adventure. It was the closest he ever came to revealing anything akin to real human emotion. Moments like those were the reason her impossible crush sometimes felt like it was veering towards something just a little bit more.

Her hand shook ever so slightly as she tucked her hair behind her ear. 'It's perfect, right? Rugged and yet accessible. And wait till you get a load of the mountain up close. You'll *never* want to leave. For me that moment will no doubt come the minute I step foot in the corner spa in my room.'

A crease, then three, dug grooves into his forehead.

Okay, so maybe she was laying it on too thick. But if he understood her enthusiasm for the place, for the project, then come Tuesday she might be in with a chance for the promotion to actual producer she'd so blithely flung out there the day before.

He put the car back into gear and curved it around the

circular drive until they pulled to a stop in front of a sweep of wide wooden stairs. Finally her holiday—read 'Bradley-free time'—could begin in earnest.

When he got out of the car at the same time as her, she gave him a double-take. It turned into a triple when she realised he wasn't dragging her luggage from the boot. He was eyeing the hotel's front doors.

Her stomach sank. She waved a frantic hand at the hotel. 'No, no, *no*! First you show up at my apartment and practically drag me here on your plane. Then you force me into that excuse for a tourist car. And now this?'

He turned to her, his eyes unreadable. 'And there I was thinking I had been *generous* in supplying a private jet and a free hire car as a way of thanking you for all your hard work.'

For half a second she felt a stab of guilt. Then she remembered that Bradley never did anything that didn't somehow serve *him*.

'Fine,' she shot back. 'Play it your way. But I can tell you now you won't get a room.'

For the first time that day she saw a flicker of doubt. So she rubbed it in good. 'Winter is peak season in this corner of the world, so the Gatehouse has been booked out for months. And, apart from the other big party here—a high-school reunion— this wedding of ours is *huge*. My mother knows everybody, Elyse is too sweet not to invite everyone she's ever met, and Tim's mother is Italian. Half the territory will be here. If they have a broom closet they'll be making a hundred bucks a night on it.'

He looked at the hotel, and at the glimpse of ragged peaks beyond. Then his jaw stiffened in the way that she knew meant he was not backing down.

His voice was smooth as honey as he said, 'You clearly have a relationship with the management. Use your magic and get me somewhere to sleep. One night to see this mountain you have raved so much about. And then you won't see me for dust.'

The temptation to wield her organisational magic in order to have him on his way the next day was mighty powerful. But after the day she'd had she didn't trust him as far as she could throw him.

'I'm. On. Holiday. You want a room? *You* go in there and make it happen.'

'Are you intimating I can't even book a hotel room without you holding my hand?'

Hannah tried hard to get the image of holding Bradley's anything out of her mind.

'I'm not intimating anything. I'm telling you outright.' She rubbed her arms and shivered theatrically. 'It gets dark quick around here this time of year. Cold too. And you're still a good two hours to Queenstown. Old copper mine. A couple of old motor inns there. You might just luck out.'

She heaved open the boot and dragged her luggage free. By the time it plopped at her feet she realised Bradley had eaten up the distance between them till they stood toe to toe.

She crossed her arms. 'You won't get a room.'

'Want to bet?'

Hannah wasn't a gambler by nature. She had an aversion to nasty surprises. But the odds were so completely in her favour. When Elyse had told her about Great-Aunt Maude's absence she'd called the hotel, and they'd all but cried with relief at being able to give her room to someone on the list of people desperate for it. Bradley would be driving on within the hour.

'Sure,' she said, a sly smile stretching across her face. 'I'm game.'

'Excellent. Now, we need to talk terms of the bet. What's in play? Ladies first.'

She thought about asking for an extra week off, at his expense. Now she was here, now she'd survived seeing her mum, it seemed like something she might be able to handle. It seemed like something she might need.

But it was unlikely she was ever going to get a chance as good as this to beat him at something. She had to make the most of it. 'I get co-producer credit if you make a show here.'

Bradley's forehead creases were back with a vengeance. Everything suddenly felt all too quiet. She could hear her own breaths gaining speed. Her heart-rate was rocketing all over the place. She wondered if she'd just screwed everything up royally.

Then she thought again. She *deserved* a producer credit, considering the amount of input she'd had in his productions to date. And if this was what it took for him to realise she meant more to his organisation than a way with middle management...

'Deal,' he said.

'Really?' she squeaked, jumping up and down on the spot as if firecrackers were exploding beneath her feet. She swished a hand across the sky as if she was looking at a podium at an awards ceremony. 'I can see it now: *co-produced by Hannah Gillespie*. "And the award goes to Hannah Gillespie and Bradley Knight."'

'Don't you mean Bradley Knight and Hannah Gillespie?'

'These things are always alphabetical.'

'Mmm.' He raised an eyebrow. 'And if I *do* get a room?'

'You won't.'

He grabbed his leather bag and her heavy suitcase and walked towards the hotel as though he was carrying a bag of feathers. She hurried after him.

'Bradley? The terms?'

'What does it matter? You're so sure I'm not going to win.'

He shot her a grin. An all too rare teeth and crinkly eyes

grin. Butterflies fluttered in her stomach. Big, broad-winged, jungle butterflies.

He wouldn't win. There was just no way. But this was Bradley Knight. So long as she'd known him—whether it was getting the green light on every show he pitched, getting any time slot he wanted, or keeping his private life private—he *always* got his way.

She jogged up the steps, puffing. He took them two at a time as if it was nothing. At the top he slowed, opened the door, and waved her through. She shot him a sarcastic smile and, head held high, walked inside.

Two steps in, they came to a halt as one. Hannah breathed out hard as she realised with immense relief that the Gatehouse was as beautiful as she'd hoped it would be. All marble floors and exposed beams and fireplaces the size of an elephant. It was fit for kings. But not Knights. No Knights.

'Stunning,' he said.

'And fully booked,' Hannah added.

Bradley laughed, the deep sound reverberating in the large open space. 'You are one stubborn creature, Miss Gillespie. I do believe it would behove me to remember that.'

She couldn't help but smile back.

Until he said, 'I'm coming to your sister's wedding.'

'I'm sorry? What?'

'If I get a room tonight it would be a waste not to thoroughly check out this part of the world. And if I'm here it would be the height of rudeness not to take up your sister's invitation.'

'And the hits just keep on coming!'

His eyes gleamed with the last vestiges of a smile. 'Are we on?'

The jungle butterflies in her stomach were wiped out by a rush of liquid heat that invaded her whole system. Red flags sprang up in its wake, but the prize was simply too big to back down now.

'We're on.'

He narrowed determined eyes, looked around, then took her by the shoulders and aimed her at the bar. 'Give me five minutes.'

'What the heck? I'll give you twenty.'

As she headed to the bar his laughter followed like a wave of warmth that sent goosebumps trailing up and down her spine.

She plonked onto a barstool in the gorgeous, sparsely populated lounge bar. In twenty minutes' time she'd know if she'd bet her way into a promotion, or if her impossible boss was coming to her little sister's wedding.

Either way she needed a drink.

Hannah let the maraschino cherry from the garnish of her soul-warming Boston Sour slide around inside her mouth a while before biting blissfully down. A pianist in the far corner was tinkling out a little Bee Gees, and the view from the twelve-foot windows was picture-postcard-perfect.

She sighed as the whisky worked its magic. And finally, for the first time since she'd headed off that morning, she began to unwind enough to feel as if she was really on holiday.

'Hannah Banana!'

She spun, to find Elyse barrelling her way. Her eyes instantly searched over her sister's shoulder, but thankfully Elyse was alone.

Elyse threw herself into Hannah's arms and hugged tight. 'Isn't this place gorgeous? You were *soooo* right in suggesting it. Tim and I owe you big-time!'

Hannah hugged back, at first in surprise. But soon she found it felt familiar, and really nice. She closed her eyes and a million small memories came flooding back to the surface. Sharing bedrooms. Sharing dolls. Sharing a secretly pilfered tube of their mum's lipstick to paint their dolls' faces. Memories she'd purposely tucked far away in order to make the move from Tasmania to Melbourne a completely fresh start.

'It's the least I could do,' Hannah said, eventually patting Elyse on the back and pulling away before it began to feel too nice. 'Considering I couldn't do much proper bridesmaid stuff from the other side of the pond.'

'You did just grand. Best maid of honour ever.' Elyse's eyes were already sweeping the big empty room. 'So where's your gorgeous man?'

'Off to chat up the management,' Hannah said, without thinking. She felt herself pinking and glanced into her drink. 'But he's not my *man*. He's my boss. And he's here to work.'

Elyse's perfectly plucked eyebrows disappeared under her perfectly straight fringe. 'So it's pure coincidence that you came on the exact same plane? And that of all the places in all the world he *had* to be today it was Cradle Mountain? The man has ulterior motive written all over him!'

Hannah coughed out a laugh. Her little sister might still look as if butter wouldn't melt in her mouth, but the girl was all grown up. 'Believe me, there is less than nothing going on between me and Bradley Knight.'

Elyse leaned her elbows on the bar and tapped the floor in front with a pointed toe—an old habit from long-ago ballet training. 'So he's not here because he's secretly in love with you and is afraid you're going to run away with the best man and leave him broken-hearted?'

This time Hannah's laughter was uproarious. 'I'm sorry to break your romantic little heart, but Bradley would be more likely to fear a sudden departure on my end would leave him with no dry-cleaning.'

She glanced out through the arched doorway to see the man in question still leaning on the reception counter. His dark wavy hair curled slightly over the back of the wool collar of his leather jacket. His jeans accentuated every nature-hewn muscle. Even from that distance the man was so beautiful he almost shimmered—like a mirage.

She glanced at the guy behind the reception counter and smiled to herself. If he'd managed to land a woman she might have begun to worry her bet was on shaky ground.

'So he's not coming to the wedding, then?'

Hannah dragged her eyes back to Elyse, smile still well in place. 'I'm afraid not. It was sweet of you to ask. But he really does have to work. He's a workaholic. Big-time. Should have the word tattooed on his forehead. If they made marrying one's job legal, he'd beat you to the altar.'

When she realised she was rambling, she put down her drink and with one finger pushed it out of reach.

A glutton for punishment, she looked back towards Reception in time to find Bradley's eyes scanning the massive foyer. They angled towards the bar and stopped.

He was too far away for her to be sure, but she knew he had her in his sights. She could feel it as if a laser had pierced her stomach, burning her up from the inside out. The piano music and the chatter of newly arrived guests spilling into the bar became a blur of white noise behind the thump, thump, thump of her heart.

Bradley gave her a slight nod. All she could do was swallow. There was so much blood rushing to her face it felt numb.

'Anyhoo,' Elyse said, 'everything's going like clockwork. So tonight no organising from you. Just party! Okay?'

Hannah frowned at her toes a moment, before lifting her head with a bright smile. 'Party sounds great.'

'Now, my love bunny and I haven't seen one another all day, and the poor pet will be fretting. I'd best head up to our room and ease his mind.'

With a wink that told of salacious goings on, Elyse flounced off.

Elyse—all grown-up and irreverent with it. Her mother—not unhappy to see her. A pleasant kind of warmth that had nothing to do with flickering fires or Boston Sours or even Bradley Knight began to spread through her.

Until a hotel room key slid in front of Hannah's face, with Bradley's long, tanned fingers on the other end.

'What is *that*?' she asked, her drink threatening to come back out the way it had gone in.

'Do you really need to ask?' Bradley drawled as he slid around behind her, the lapels of his jacket brushing against her back, causing her spine to roll in delicious anguish, before he straddled the bar stool beside her.

She spun on her seat to glare at him. Her knees knocked his before he shifted, placing a hand on her knee and allowing it to tuck neatly between his. Even then he didn't let go—just rested a hand there as if it was nothing.

As cool as she could manage, Hannah said, 'If you promised the man your firstborn son you've lost all my respect.'

The smile in his eyes gave her hot chills. As if she was sitting on the edge of a volcano. The kind from which you knew you ought to flee if only you could just let go of the primal urge to jump right in.

'I didn't do anything drastic,' he said. 'Or illegal. I simply negotiated. The only way I could get a room was to get us a suite.'

'I'm sorry, did you say *us*?'

Bradley glanced at the bartender, who poured a fresh packet of peanuts into a small glass bowl. 'Separate rooms off a shared lounge. Better even than the honeymoon suite, or so I've been told.'

While he was crowing, she was fast turning to a wobbly mess. But what could she say? They'd shared suites on numerous occasions before—at TV trade fairs or in pre-production on new shows—using the joint lounge as a makeshift office. Of course they'd been constantly surrounded by the half-dozen odd staff who travelled everywhere with him. Who were right now in New Zealand.

Her unimpressed air must have been crystal-clear, because he added, 'From what I heard they only let the Platinum Suite to their most favoured VIPs.' She narrowed her eyes. 'That's my mother's suite. I had to schmooze like crazy to make sure she got that room in the first place.'

Something that seemed a heck of a lot like a blush washed across Bradley's face. But Hannah was too infuriated to take any heed.

'I bumped into Virginia at the desk. She overheard my predicament and offered to swap rooms. She now has your single, and we have her suite.'

Hannah had her face in her hands and was rocking on her chair by that stage.

Bradley's thumb curving over her knee brought her out of her trance. She ran her hands down her face and did her best to act as though it was irrelevant that he was touching her at all.

She turned to glare at him, only to find glints throwing out specks of silver in his dark grey eyes. He said, 'Turns out that despite Virginia's predilection for…what was it?'

'Pink cardigans and cocktails with umbrellas in them,' she muttered.

'That's right. I couldn't remember beyond rhinestones. It turns out that she's an entirely sensible woman.'

Sensible? *Sensible?*

'Oh, no, no, *no*,' Hannah said, waggling a furious finger in front of his face. 'Don't *you* go falling for her act. Virginia is the very opposite of sensible. She's a narcissistic, selfish, hurtful creature who *always* has an agenda. And it always revolves around how any situation can benefit *her*.'

Her harsh words seemed to echo in the large space, coming back at her and back at her, like some kind of horrible Groundhog Day moment.

Bradley's hand slipped away from her knee and she felt

the cool slap of his silence. She hunched her shoulders in mortification and stared unseeingly at a patch of carpet.

'Evidently,' he drawled into the painful silence, 'until this moment I wasn't aware just how deeply the issues run between your mother and you.'

She ran her fingers through her hair, needing to shake off the crazies. 'Well, now you are.'

Suddenly Hannah felt very, very tired. As if her years in the city, working her backside off, building an impeccable professional reputation, creating a life for herself from nothing, doing her best to forget the period of her life at home after her dad died, were catching up with her in one fell swoop.

With a groan, she let her head fall to the bar with a thunk.

Out of the corner of her eye she saw Bradley's fingers fiddling with the room key. Maybe one good thing had come from her pyscho rant. Maybe he was realising the level of drama he'd be subjecting himself to by standing anywhere near a Gillespie girl in full flight. Maybe he was thinking of leaving her and her mad family in peace.

She lifted her head and swept her hair from her eyes. He was looking into the middle distance, the expression in his eyes pure steel. Whatever he was thinking there would be no talking him out of it.

She breathed in deep and waited.

Finally he turned to face her, and said, 'I'm coming to your sister's wedding.'

She moved to let her head thunk against the bar again—only this time he saw it coming. He took her by the shoulders, holding her upright. She wobbled like a marionette.

She must have looked as pathetic and wretched as she felt because his hands slid to cradle her neck, to slip beneath her hair, his thumbs touching the soft spots just below her ears. He had to be able to feel her pulse thundering in her neck at his gentle but insistent touch, but he didn't show it.

He just looked her right in the eye—serious, determined, beautiful. 'By the sound of things you're walking into a lions' den this weekend, with no back-up. It wouldn't be showing you any kind of thanks for having my back all these months if I just walked away and let that happen. Especially after exacerbating the problem. I'll be your wing man.'

His hands dropped to her shoulders, and then away.

Hannah wondered if a person could get jet lag from a one-hour flight. Because, blinking slowly at Bradley's mouth, that was just how she felt—woozy, off-kilter, slipping in and out of a parallel universe. Surely the fact that Bradley Knight had just offered to be her *wing man* was a hallucination.

She glanced at her drink. It was still three-quarters full.

'Hannah—'

She closed her tired eyes and held up a hand. 'I'm thinking.'

'About?'

About the fact that she couldn't twist his offer to mean anything other than what it meant. There was no punishment for rhinestone comparisons at play. By offering to throw himself in the path of the drama tornado, for *her*, he was being nice. Thoughtful. Selfless. Things she'd taken pains to remind herself he was not.

She took a deep breath and said, 'It's a really nice offer, Bradley. Truly. But this holiday is not all about my family. It's about taking a break from work…and those I work with.'

She glanced up at him with one eye open.

Taciturn, stoic, unreadable as ever, he said, 'Meaning me?'

She opened the other eye and nodded. 'You. And Sonja. And dealing with prima donnas all day. And Spencer following me around like a lovesick puppy while I'm trying to work. And sixty-hour weeks. And no sleeping-in—'

'Okay. I get it. I hadn't realised you found your job such a hardship.'

Grrr! That one man could be so smart one minute and so dumb the next...

Hannah shuffled on her stool. 'Don't be daft. I love my job. More than anything else in my life. Truly. But in order to do it right I need to recharge. This weekend is my chance.'

Finally, after such a long time she wondered if he'd heard a word of what she'd said, he nodded. 'Fair enough.'

Then, after an even more interminable silence, he said, 'But I know how even the most...thorny of families can have the kind of pull over you nothing else can. And that doesn't mean you have to take their crap. Not alone, anyway. If that's a concern in your case, my offer stands.'

She let out a great fat sigh. And, whether it was from the shock of his little insight, or a masochistic streak she was becoming all too familiar with, she threw her hands in the air and said, 'Fine. Okay.'

'Okay?' He perked up. As if he was finding himself quite enjoying playing the hero.

It was irresistible. *He* was irresistible. And he was going to be her plus one at her sister's wedding.

She was in mounds and mounds of trouble.

He took her hand, slipped it into the crook of his elbow and helped her off the stool.

'Come on, kiddo, let's go see what's so amazing about the suites in this place.'

'Prepare to have your socks literally knocked off.'

Glancing up at him as they walked through Reception, arm in arm, her blood fizzing more and more every time her hip bumped against his, she saw an ever so slight curve to his mouth.

Mounds and mounds and mounds of trouble.

CHAPTER FIVE

The lift doors opened to reveal a line of people outside the Gatehouse's basement nightclub. The *doof-doof-doof* of the beat echoing from behind the bouncer-manned double doors thundered in Hannah's chest.

It didn't help that she was overly aware of the big warm man standing so close behind her she could feel the brush of his jeans against her backside every time the line moved.

'Stop fidgeting,' Bradley said, his breath brushing her chandelier earring against her bare neck. 'You look fine.'

'Thanks,' she said dryly. But she could hardly tell him the fidgets were all his doing.

The doors opened. Lights flashed over their faces. The line moved forward. Hannah took her chance and arched away from him. The doors closed. *Doof-doof-doof.*

'I was serious when I said you should get a guide to take you out for a night tour of Cradle Mountain rather than coming along to this pre-wedding party thing.'

'I'm fine.'

'Look,' she said, leaning back so she could drop her voice in case any of the bouncy young things in line were from Elyse's wedding party, 'it's just going to be a bunch of locals, all of whom will pinch me on the cheek and remind me they were there the time I took off down Main Street naked. You'll be bored out of your mind.'

When he didn't answer straight away she looked up at him,

surprised to find his jaw was clenched. He asked, 'You took off down Main Street naked?'

The husky timbre of his voice gave her pause before she cleared her throat and explained, 'I was two, and not overly keen on having a bath that evening.'

The slightly haunted look in his eyes disappeared. 'You were a tearaway?'

'Hardly. I was the perfect first child. Studious, polite, a pleaser. I took singing and dancing lessons for four years because Mum wanted me to—even though I'm tone deaf with two left feet. In compensation, when I did have my moments, I made the most of them—usually in front of the entire town.'

'Coming in?' the bouncer asked.

Hannah looked up to find they were at the front of the line. And she was still leaning back against her boss as though they were in the middle of a crushing crowd.

She pulled herself upright, rolled her shoulders and said, 'You betcha.'

The bouncer smiled. 'Knock 'em dead.'

Hannah gave him a bright smile, feeling for the first time that night as if maybe she could. As if she was no longer the naked two-year-old, or the gawky, soccer-playing tomboy kid of the local beauty queen. 'You know what? I'm going to do just that.'

The guy cleared his throat and blushed.

Only when she nodded did he open the door.

Bradley placed his hand against the small of her back and gave her a not too subtle shove. In fact she practically had to trot to stop from falling over.

'Somebody has a fan,' Bradley murmured against her ear once they were inside and the *doof-doof-doof* had become music so loud she could barely hear herself.

'I do not.'

'That big, burly bouncer back there thinks you look more

than fine tonight. He thinks you look downright gorgeous. And you know what?'

Hannah was feeling so dizzy from the effects of that voice skimming her ear she was amazed she had the ability to speak. 'What?'

'He has a point.'

Then the door swung shut behind them, and it was too loud to do anything but shout to be heard.

The club was rocking. Tasmania-style.

There were men with burnt-orange copper mine dust stained into their jeans and the grooves of their hands, mixed with women and men in business suits, twenty-somethings in classic black club attire, and tourists in sensible layers.

And then there was Hannah.

Bradley might not have been to a wedding in his life, but he had seen his fair share of bachelor parties. Leaving studious, polite and pleasing Hannah to her own devices at such a do, looking the way she did, was never going to happen.

Smoky make-up and glossy pink lips. Tousled hair that seemed to shimmer every time she moved. And an outfit that seemed demure at first glance only to cling in all the right places the second she breathed.

Not that his imagination needed help. All that talk of her running naked down Main Street had brought her dash from the bathroom back to the front and centre of his mind. In full 3D. Technicolor. As for her perfume... It had his nostrils flaring like a horse in heat every time she moved.

If she'd come to the wilds of Tasmania looking for a wild fling then she was going the right way about it. Hell, without even turning his head he could see a dozen men checking her out, and the look in their eyes was creating a red mist behind his.

Because *he* had her back. He'd promised he would, and he was a man of his word.

He moved in closer, putting his hands on her shoulders as

she began to snake a path through the club, so he wouldn't lose her in the crowd. Her hair spilled over his fingers, silky soft. His thumbs rested against the back of her warm neck.

The fact that those men with room keys burning holes in their pockets might consider his touch some kind of brand was their problem.

And possibly, he admitted, his.

It would only take one of those goons to show her the time of her life this long weekend and she'd have reason to wonder if sixty-hour weeks working for a stubborn perfectionist was actually a form of sado-masochism.

Resolve turned to steel inside him. Hannah must have felt it in his grip. She glanced back at him, eyebrows raised in question. He tilted his head towards the bar, and lifted a hand off her shoulder to motion that he needed a drink.

She gave him a thumbs-up and a wide, bright smile. Even in the smoky half-darkness the luminosity in those eyes of hers cut through. Showing the lightness of spirit that made her easy to have around.

The goons could go hang. She'd be damned hard to replace.

The crowd bumped and jostled. Then out of nowhere lumbered a guy carrying a tray of beers who looked as if he'd drunk a keg by himself already that night. Instinctively Bradley slid an arm around Hannah's slight waist and lifted her bodily to one side. She squeaked as she avoided having a cup of beer spilled over her in its entirety by about half a hair's breadth.

He found a breathing space in the gap around a massive pillar covered in trails of fake ivy, and let her down slowly until her back was against the protective sconce.

His breaths came heavily. Then again, so did hers. Her chest lifting and falling, her lips slightly parted. Pupils so dark he couldn't find a lick of green.

A wisp of hair was stuck to her cheek. He casually swept

the strand back into place, tucking it behind her ear where he knew she liked it. But there was nothing casual about the sudden burst of energy that coursed through his finger, as if he'd had an electric shock. He folded his fingers into his palm.

'You're making a habit of coming to my rescue this weekend,' she said, shifting until the hand that had remained on her hip nudged at her hipbone. 'A girl could get used to it.'

'Don't,' he growled, shocked at the ferocity of the urge to slide his hand up to her waist to see if it was as soft and warm as the sliver of skin he touched indicated. 'I'm no Galahad. I was thinking of myself the whole time. Of the griping I'd have to put up with if you ended up soaked head to toe in beer.'

He pictured it now. *Her skin glistening. Her white top rendered all but see-through. Her tongue sliding between her lips to clean away the amber fluid shining thereupon.*

He'd never felt himself grow so hard so fast.

But this was Hannah. The woman whose job it was to de-complicate his life. Hannah, whose hair smelt of apples. Whose soft pink lips were parted so temptingly. Who was looking up at him with those wide, bright and clear open eyes of hers. Unblinking. Unflinching. Unshrinking.

He stood his ground for several beats, then slowly, carefully, removed his hands from her body, sliding one into a safe spot in the back pocket of his jeans and placing the other on the column above her head.

'Now,' he said, his voice as deep as an ocean, 'do you still want that drink?'

She nodded, her hair spilling sexily over her shoulders. It took every ounce of his strength not to wrap his fingers around a lock and tug her the last few inches it would take for those wide, soft pink lips to meet his.

'Boston Sour, right?' he asked.

She nodded again. A waft of that killer perfume slid past

his nose. He gripped the pillar so hard he felt plaster come away on his fingernails.

'I'm guessing beer for you,' Hannah said. 'Imported. Sliver of lime.'

Her words carried a slow smile, and behind that a hesitant note of flirtation he'd never heard from her before. He knew her drink of choice. She knew his. And now they both knew it.

'Stay here,' he demanded. 'Don't move. I didn't save you from that booze-soaked clod so that some other mischief might befall you the second I leave you alone.'

He'd moved to push away, to get her drink and whatever they could pour quickest for himself, when she lifted a hand and flicked an imaginary speck from his shirt. 'Whether you want to admit it or not, beneath the tough guy exterior you are, in fact, an honest-to-goodness nice guy.'

Through the cotton of his shirt her fingernails scraped against the hair on his chest, which sprang to attention at her touch. He clenched his teeth so hard a shot of pain pulsed in his temple.

Nice? Hardly. The truth was her tough relationship with her mother had unexpectedly slid beneath his defences and connected with his own. And in a rare fit of solidarity he'd felt he had no choice but to help.

He wasn't being nice. He was choosing sides in battle. A battle whose lines were fast blurring. Dangerously fast.

It was time to make the boundaries perfectly clear. So that she understood just how close to the fire they were dancing.

'Honey,' he drawled, 'looking out for you this weekend is purely professional insurance. I want you back on dry land this Tuesday, ready to work—not all hung-over and homesick, addled by wedding-induced romantic thoughts. That's it. End of story. You think your mother is egocentric? She has nothing on me.'

He dropped his hand till it rested just above her shoulder.

Edged closer till she had to arch back to look him in the eye. Till his knee brushed against the outside of hers. The rasp of denim on suede shot sparks up his leg which settled with a painful fizz in his groin.

She flinched at the sliding contact. Her cheeks grew red. The crowd jostled, the music blared, and the air around them was so heavy with implication and consequence it vibrated. He was meant to be teaching his protégée a lesson. Instead the effort of keeping himself in check made his muscles burn.

Hannah's hand slowly flattened to rest against his chest. But she didn't push him away. If the thunderous thumping of his heart wasn't enough of a caution to her, he wondered how far he might have to go.

And where the point of no return might be.

It did occur to him—far too late—that he might have walked blithely past it the moment he'd stepped off his plane. The moment he'd made certain they'd be stranded on an island, to all intents and purposes alone.

Suddenly she gave him a hearty shove, then ducked under his arm and took off to the edge of the dance floor. He should have been relieved. But it wasn't often he had a girl literally bolt from his advances—simulated or otherwise.

Feeling suddenly adrift, he made to follow when the strains of a new song blaring over the speakers stopped him short. That particular combination of notes plucked at something inside him. Something that chased all of Hannah's latent heat from his veins and chilled him to the bone.

In his mind's eye he could see a woman standing at a kitchen bench, hand reaching out for an overly full glass of wine, dishtowel thrown over her shoulder, gently swaying from side to side as she quietly sang along with the small radio on the bench at her elbow.

One of his aunts? No. Wrong kitchen.

The woman in his mind turned, but he couldn't see her face. In the end he didn't need to. The moment she saw him her whole body seemed to contract in on itself, and the overwhelming sense of rebuff told him exactly who she was.

It was his mother's kitchen. His mother's disappointment bombarding him. Telling him without words that he was nothing to her but a constant reminder that she'd fallen pregnant young and his father had bolted the minute he'd heard. It was *his* fault her life hadn't tuned out as she'd hoped it would.

'No, no, *no*!' a familiar voice shouted at the edge of his consciousness.

He dragged himself back to the present to see Hannah, in her tight capri pants, sexy stilettos, hair tumbling down her back, with hands to her ears, mouth agape, staring into the distance.

At the sight of her—the realness of her, the *now*ness of her—the unbearable memory dissolved like a pinch of salt in a pool of water. It was just what he needed in that moment. *She* was just what he needed.

'Are you okay?' he asked, placing a hand on her arm. Hannah's warmth beneath his fingers further banished the cold memories. Selfishly, he let his hand trail down her arm till it found purchase in the sultry dip of her waist.

At his intimate touch her eyes snapped from the middle distance to glance at him. Cheeks pink. Eyes bright and questioning. Confused.

But mostly curious.

His solar plexus clenched in pure and unadulterated sexual response. It hit so hard, so violently, he just had to stand there and ride it. Either that or haul her over his shoulder like some caveman and drag her back to their room. Their shared room.

The song changed key. Hannah blinked, as if coming round from a trance. Then she waved a frantic arm in the direction of the karaoke stage and yelled to be heard over the speakers buzzing nearby. 'I'm not tall enough to see, but is that my mother?'

Her mother?

'You mean the one singing?'

Hannah nodded frantically.

Bradley searched the hazy room to see Hannah's mother was indeed up on stage, belting out a Cliff Richard classic while swinging her hips and waving at the small crowd who were cheering as if she was a rock star. A man joined her on stage—a man young enough to be Hannah's brother. Though from the way they oozed over the microphone together Bradley assumed the man was *not* blood-related.

'That would be her,' he said, keeping that last part to himself.

The sad, withdrawn, silently accusing woman fading in his mind and Hannah's effervescent mother couldn't have been more diametrically opposite if they'd tried. But neither of them could ever have hoped to be named mother of the year.

Instinct moved him closer to Hannah still. His body protecting hers from the crush. When she didn't pull away he slid his arm further around her waist, drawing her close enough that he collected wafts of that insanely sexy perfume with every breath. Then she leaned into him, the curves of her body slotting so temptingly into the grooves of his, and a slow, steady pulse began to throb in his groin.

Who was playing with fire now?

'Come on, kiddo,' he shouted above the din. 'Let's get those drinks.'

They hadn't taken two steps when they were stopped by a small crowd of people and Hannah was wrenched from Bradley, leaving a chill where her sensual warmth had been.

He shoved his untrustworthy hands back in pockets, and watched as person after person grabbed Hannah in a warm embrace. She was right; her naked run down Main Street *was* well-remembered.

After a minute Hannah sent him a look of apology. He shook

his head once to tell her it was fine. And it was. Watching someone else get mobbed rather than him was something of a novelty.

Attention always made him feel scratchy. He'd never courted it, never coveted it, and certainly hadn't done anything to deserve it. Even if he had, the attention was so foreign he'd never been equipped to know how to deal with it bar turning to stone till the discomfort passed.

Hannah, on the other hand, took attention and affection in her stride. As if it was expected. As if it was her right.

A completely unexpected kick of something that felt a whole lot like envy tightened his throat.

He'd never cared that not one of the folk who'd been forced to take him in had ever come looking for him. Not even since he'd found some notoriety. In fact he'd been relieved. If he couldn't put on an act for complete strangers, there was no way he could have done so for them.

But watching Hannah glow and blush and laugh, revelling in the close company of those who'd been witness to her life, gave him a glimpse at the other side of the looking glass. The sense of belonging he'd never been allowed to have.

This was what she'd walked away from. What she could have again if she ever chose to come home for good.

As if to jab the point home deep, Elyse leapt into the crowd surrounding Hannah, yanking her from the fray and back to his side. She shouted over the crowd noise, 'I want to introduce you to someone!'

With a sweeping motion Elyse invited another man into their circle. Light brown hair, dimples, arms like a wrestler, twenty-five if he was a day. Elyse's fiancé, Bradley assumed. They suited one another. A pair of happy-go-lucky puppies.

'This is Hannah,' Elyse said, wrapping her arm about Hannah's shoulder, her gleaming eyes glancing hungrily between Hannah and... Not Tim, Bradley realised all too late, when he saw the predatory gleam in the other man's eyes.

'I'm Roger,' said Dimples. 'The best man. Elyse, you were being miserly when you described how pretty she was.' Behind his hand he stage-whispered, 'Your sister's a knockout.'

Elyse laughed uproariously and pinched Hannah on the arm. Hannah did her best to pretend she hadn't noticed. Bradley felt a distinctly non-puppy-like growl building inside him.

'Pleased to meet you, Roger,' Hannah said, holding out a hand.

Dimples took it—and kissed it.

Elyse clapped.

Hannah smiled politely.

Bradley stood to his full height and thought weightlifting-type thoughts.

Elyse must have noticed him filling every inch of available space, and gave a perfunctory wave in his direction. 'Roger, this is Bradley Knight—Hannah's boss. He's filling in for Great-Aunt Maude.'

Bradley deflated, not sure he'd ever been given a more underwhelming introduction.

The two men shook hands. Dimples held on a little too tight. *Punk.* Bradley gave the kid one last ominous squeeze before letting go. He couldn't hide his smile when the guy winced.

Lightweight.

'I hear you're an aerobics instructor?' Bradley said.

'Personal trainer,' Roger shot back, seemingly oblivious to the intended put-down.

Hannah, on the other hand, noticed very much. In fact she gave a little cough at the exact time she stamped on Bradley's foot with one of those damned stiletto heels. He shook out his pulsating foot, then shoved his shoe neatly between hers. Her heels slid apart on the parquetry floor, and a hard breath puffed through her lips.

As Elyse waxed lyrical about the hotel, Hannah's hand

drifted behind her to rest against his thigh. He clenched every-where while he waited to see what she might do in retribution. As it turned out the gentle rise and fall of her pinky finger against his leg as she breathed was punishment enough.

'And, boy, can your mum sing! Am I right?' Roger said, giving Hannah a chummy punch on her arm.

Hannah blinked as though she'd forgotten he was even there. 'Pardon? Oh, yeah. That she can!'

'She was singing in a nightclub when our parents first met,' Elyse piped up. 'She was practising for her Miss Tasmania pageant number. He requested "The Way You Look Tonight", which is her favourite song ever. It was love at first sight.'

'Sounds like your father was a smart man,' Roger said, sidling closer to Hannah.

Bradley had to stop himself from hauling her out of the guy's way. A hard stare had to suffice.

Though Roger, it seemed, wasn't as much of a meat-head as he'd first appeared. He shot Bradley a grin. A take-me-on-if-you-dare-Grandpa kind of grin.

'Do you too have the voice of a nightingale?' Roger asked, shining his dimples Hannah's way.

Hannah waved her hands frantically in front of her face. 'No. Nope. God, no. Uh-uh. No way. Tone deaf. Allergic to microphones. Rabid stage-fright.'

'So that's a no, then?'

Hannah laughed. 'That would be a gigantic no.'

Roger grinned.

Elyse did a little happy jig.

Before he even knew what he was about to do, Bradley reached out and tucked his fingers around the belt of Hannah's pants. His nails grazed the curve at the top of her buttocks. She all but leapt from her tottering shoes before she pressed her hand over his.

He fully expected her to slap his hand away. Or to do worse damage with her lethal shoes. He wouldn't have blamed her.

His move had been so far over the line of propriety it was nothing short of reckless.

But after a moment, two, her hand still remained locked over his. If anything she'd melted closer. Until he was near enough to see her neck was turning pink. To feel the heavy rise and fall of her breaths. To be gripped by the scent of her perfume.

As far as adventure thrills went, that moment was right up there. It was indecent. Torturously tempting. And, with no exit strategy in sight, completely against his own best interests.

He wondered quite how far he could go in the flickering semi-darkness, with her sister and Dimples and half her home town watching on. And how far this vamp version of Hannah would let him. His throbbing pulse ramped up into such a frenzy he could barely see straight.

'Speak of the devil,' Elyse said, and the unexpected angst in the girl's voice was so potent it hauled him back to the present with a snap.

As one they turned to face the distant karaoke stage where the strains of 'The Way You Look Tonight' rang out in Virginia's distinctively husky tones.

With his hand still tucked decadently into her pants, Bradley felt Hannah stiffen. The deliciously dark overtones to their play chilled. No guesses as to why. Virginia was singing the forties torch song her daughters associated with their deceased father. And she was singing it with yet another man.

From out of nowhere fury enveloped him. Fury he could barely control.

He moved himself in closer to Hannah, feeling a need to say…he knew not what, exactly. That he understood her disappointment? That he'd felt it too? That the only way to survive it was to turn your insides to rock so hard no amount of chipping made a dent?

No, he wouldn't say any of that. Couldn't. Not even while she practically crumbled before his eyes.

Besieged by a swirl of raw emotion, this was usually the point where he'd begin to feel icicles forming in his blood.

But then Hannah murmured, quietly enough he was sure only he heard, 'Please, God, somebody remind her that this is her daughter's wedding—not the place to pick up her next ex-husband.'

And he felt as if a pair of huge cold hands was squeezing his chest.

The adventure of the moment had been overtaken by too much stark reality for his liking.

He slid his hand from Hannah's back and moved out of the circle. He clapped his hands loud enough that the small group turned his way. 'Who wants a drink? My shout.'

'There's a bar tab, silly,' Elyse said.

'Even better. So, for the bride?'

'Black Russian.'

'Excellent. Beer for me. Boston Sour for Hannah.'

'Hey, that was Dad's favourite drink,' Elyse said.

Bradley glanced at Hannah. With a deep breath she turned away from the stage and into the conversation. 'The man had great taste—with only the occasional slip.'

Her eyes slid to his, a warm flicker coming back to life within. He couldn't drag his eyes away even as he said, 'Roger? Your favourite drink is…?'

'I'd kill for a tequila slammer,' Roger piped up.

The warmth in Hannah's eyes sparked into a flickering fire, and her mouth turned up at the corners as she stifled a laugh. She had a great smile. Infectious as all get out. Bradley felt his own cheeks lifting in response.

'Now, Roger, while you await your tequila slammer you should ask Hannah about her naked run down Main Street. It's a classic.'

Hannah's smile disappeared as she gawped at him—all hot pink cheeks and pursed red lips, bright eyes and huffing chest. Then she slowly shook her head. A warning of reprisals to come.

It was with that image in mind—that dark promise—that he turned and headed for the bar.

What a difference a day makes.

It had been less than a day since thought of Hannah jetting off for a wild weekend and a family wedding on an island she clearly adored had finally spooked him enough to abandon a long-planned New Zealand research trip on a plane.

Checking out Tasmania was a smart business move, but there was no avoiding the fact that the timing purely came down to his need to keep an eye on her. For losing her from the team at that point in time was exactly the kind of drama he did not need.

What with the Argentina show all but ready to fly, and New Zealand well and truly in the works. And now the germ of a new idea about Tasmania. He didn't have the time to break in someone new.

He found a spot at the bar where he was a head taller than every other patron. Three rows back, he still caught the eye of a bored-looking barmaid. She perked up, fixed her hair, smiled, and ignored the throng between them.

He boomed out his order and mimed his room number for the bill. She pretended to write it on her hand. Or maybe she wasn't pretending. She was cute. Willing. Lived miles away. But no part of him was stirred. Literally. Odd…

Drinks ordered, his thoughts readily skidded back to where he'd left them.

Breaking in a new employee was always frustrating. Not Hannah. She'd been a breeze from day one. With the stamina to keep up with him, the temperament to handle him, and a light-hearted nature that made her popular with staff, crew and station management alike. She could have said *Yes, Bradley, you're right, Bradley,* a tad more for his liking—rather than contradicting him so readily. But all in all Team Bradley was the better for having her.

He was smart enough to know it wouldn't last. Nothing ever did. One day she'd move on. It was the natural order of things. Every man for himself. No exceptions. Not for promises. Not even for blood.

It appeared as though she was sticking around for the immediate future. Hell would freeze over before she'd realise how much she missed living near her mum. As for the lightweight best man? Nothing to fear there.

A woman's voice called out his room number. He reached over and collected the drinks. The barmaid batted her lashes and gave him an eyeful of cleavage. He gave her an appreciative smile, but nothing more. No need to raise the girl's obvious hopes.

He was a busy man. On a mission to keep his assistant on the straight and narrow and out of the way of any who sought to knock her from her current path.

Hannah's familiar laughter tinkled through the air. He turned to catch the sound. She was regaling the group with some story or another, and they were laughing their heads off. This was the Hannah he wasn't ready to see go. Easy. Uncomplicated. Straight up.

She tossed her head and smiled widely at someone to her left, giving him a view of her profile. She waved and laughed. Bright and vivacious. Confident and extraordinarily sexy.

Several parts of him were stirred in an instant. Dramatically.

The fact that *he* seemed to be one of those with a craving to knock her from the straight and narrow was a whole other kettle of fish.

CHAPTER SIX

HANNAH nibbled at her little fingernail until there was nothing more to nibble without taking the top off her finger.

For a weekend that was meant to be about relaxing and recharging, sorting out her head, she felt as if she'd been walking a tightrope blindfolded.

What with Elyse being so unexpectedly fabulous. Her mother driving her even crazier than she'd expected. And poor Roger flirting up a storm every chance he had while she thought him about as interesting as a potted plant.

But they were mere wallpaper compared with the most glaring factor in the story of her lack of a pinky fingernail.

What had got into Bradley?

Even thinking her boss's name had her teeth aiming for a new nail.

No matter how she played out that first half an hour inside the bar, she kept coming back to the indisputable fact that Bradley had been hitting on her. The dark glances, the whispering in her ear, the unexpected touches...

She bit down so hard on her fingernail it stung.

Wincing, she snuck a glance across the table to where the man himself sat, all six feet four inches of him, sprawled out in his chair, long fingers clasped around a glass of beer, smiling contentedly as he watched Elyse and Tim belt out 'Islands in the Stream' on the karaoke stage.

'I'm sorry?'

She blinked, realising he was leaning towards her, one eyebrow cocked, the edge of his mouth lifted in the remnants of a smile. How did the man manage to make even the word *sorry* sound so sexy?

'Did you say something?' he asked, almost shouting to be heard over the music.

'Nope. Nothing going on over here. All quiet my end.'

He looked at her a beat longer. His deep grey eyes burning into her. Heat she'd never sensed from him before was now arcing across the table and turning her knees to butter. When he finally looked away she let out a long, slow breath.

Something had shifted back there. But how much? How far? She was confused and jumpy and prickling with anticipation all at once.

Then she asked the question she'd been finding any way to avoid. Was she looking at the early stages of a fling? She gave in to a delicious shiver that tumbled through her from top to toe.

But no. No way. Anything but that. Not with the boss. She'd worked too hard to prove herself indispensable—irreplaceable, even—to turn into a cliché now.

She leant her chin on her palm and bobbed her head in time with the music, all the while watching him from the corner of her eye.

She'd have to see something way beyond fling on the horizon to even *consider* that kind of risk. Whereas Bradley... She knew first-hand that the women who dated Bradley were lucky if they stayed on his mobile phone longer than a month.

Her enigmatic, heartlessly delicious, emotionally stunted boss suddenly picked up his chair and plonked it down beside hers.

She leaned away. 'If you can't see from there I'll happily switch places.'

'Stay.' He placed a hand over hers, cupping it on the table. 'I don't plan on shouting to be heard all evening.'

She slid her hand away and used it to scratch her non-itchy head.

'Elyse is a pretty fair singer too, you know,' he drawled. 'How *did* you miss that gene?'

Hannah shook the cotton wool from her head. '*That's* what you came over here to say? Not *Are you're having a good time, Hannah?* Or *Can I get you another drink, Hannah?* But what's with the talent deficiency? You *are* a charmer.'

He laughed softly—a low rumble that whispered to all the deep, dark feminine places inside her. Serious face on, he was heart-stoppingly gorgeous. Smiling, he was devastating. Laughing, he was…a dream.

This man had been hitting on her? *Her?* Sensible, back-chatting, small-town Hannah Gillespie? She felt it, but couldn't quite believe it.

Needing to know for sure, to see if her radar was so rusty it was no longer even functional, she turned in her chair, giving him her most flirtatious smile.

'Okay,' she said, 'just so we can put this topic to bed once and for all—'

He raised an eyebrow. Her heart rate quickened. And all the places his large warm hands had glanced that night pulsed.

Hannah met his raised eyebrow and raised him another. 'I'm talking, of course, about my lack of singing and dancing skills.'

'*Riiight.*'

'I don't want you sitting there feeling all sorry for me because I can't do a series of triple-spins while belting out "I Dreamed a Dream".'

When he opened his mouth, she held up a hand. 'Before you ask, all I'll admit is that routine had fake peacock feathers and sequinned masquerade masks.'

'I was going to say that I don't feel the least bit sorry for you. A woman doesn't have to be able to sing and dance to have it going on.'

He lifted his beer and finished it in one slow swallow. All she could do was stare.

Oh, yeah. Bradley was flirting, all right. Batting her about like a lion with a moth. She wondered what she might do if he decided to stop playing and get serious. The very idea petrified her to the spot.

Even in the low light of the club she could see the gleam in his eyes. The thrill of the chase.

Utterly out of her depth, she reached for her drink.

Bradley got there first, snatching it out of her way. But not before her fingers had brushed across his. Pure and unadulterated sexual attraction wrapped itself around her like a wet rope, slippery and unyielding. And even in the darkness she was sure his pupils had grown so large the colour of his eyes was completely obscured.

From an accidental touch of fingers. Oh, God…

Bradley swirled the ice around in her drink. Once. Twice. Each time ice hit glass her nerves twanged sharply—like an out-of-tune guitar.

She sat on her hands and bit her lip. *He's your boss. You love your job. He's not looking for for ever. And you are. Just allowing this flirtation to continue is going to change everything.*

He lifted her drink to his mouth and took a sip. The press of his lips where her lips had just been made her tingle in the most aching anticipation.

Then his face screwed up as if he'd just sucked on a lemon. 'Holy heck—that's atrocious! How can you drink this slop?'

'It's not slop!'

'What on earth's in it?'

'Whisky, lemon juice, sugar, and a dash of egg white.'

'Are you *serious*?'

He picked up his empty beer glass and practically ran his

tongue around the rim in search of leftover foam. Hannah's limbs went limp so quickly she had to look away.

'It was my father's favourite drink. So clearly it's meant for a palate far more discerning than yours.'

To prove it, she put the glass to her mouth and took a giant swig—only instead of tasting the sharp mix of ingredients that had always felt nothing but warm and comforting, she was certain she could taste a whisper of beer as left by Bradley's lips.

She slammed the glass to the table, then pushed back her chair. 'I need to…do some urgent maid of honour things.'

He crossed his arms and looked at her a long time. 'Right now?'

'You know I don't like leaving things till the last minute. *Boss.*'

There. Put things back in perspective. Remind him who you are. Who he is. How things are meant to work between you.

'Need company?' A slow smile slid across his face, proving he was apparently happy to forget.

As he began to uncurl his large lanky self from the chair she backed up so fast she bumped into some poor woman who spilt her drink. Hannah pulled her emergency ten dollars from her cleavage and shoved it in the girl's hand.

Bradley sank back into the chair, his eyes glued to her décolletage as though he was wondering what other secrets she held down there. *None to write home about!* she wanted to shout.

Instead she demanded, 'Sit. Drink. Grab a lighter and sway. Whatever gets you through the night. I'll come find you later.'

And with that she spun and, head down, feet going a mile a minute, took off through any gap she could find.

Until that moment she'd enjoyed her crush on him *because* it had never had a chance of going anywhere. Bradley was impossible. Untouchable. Out of her league. In fact he'd been a convenient excuse not to get close to anyone else while she concentrated on consolidating her career.

And now?

Someone clearly cleverer than she had once said, 'Be careful what you wish for or you just might get it.'

She wished they were there right now, so she could shake their hand. Or ask if they'd mind slapping her across the back of the head as many times as it took to make sure she made it back to her bedroom that night.

Alone.

Bradley glanced at his watch to find Hannah had been AWOL for over an hour. That was as long as he'd decided to give her. Because if she was *actually* off doing maid of honour business he'd shave his head.

After five solid minutes of frustrated searching, he found her. Back against the wall in a quiet cocktail lounge at the far end of the bar. Stuck between Roger and her mother.

Even in the half-light he could see that she was struggling. Both hands were clasped tight around a tall glass of iced water as her eyes skimmed brightly from one hostage-taker to the other.

Something must have alerted her to his presence as he excused himself and made his way through the chatty crowd towards her, because her eyes shifted to lock instantly with his.

That very moment she went from dazed to delighted. Her whole face lit up as if the sun had risen inside her. It felt... nice.

'Hi,' she said on an outward breath.

He nodded.

Virginia and Roger turned in surprise, and expressed understandably different levels of excitement to see him. He gave Virginia a kiss on the cheek, and patted poor Roger on the shoulder. Poor Roger's eye began to twitch. But Bradley had more important things to worry about.

'I've been searching for you for some time,' he said.

Hannah's eyes widened in a plea for help. 'I've been right *here* for quite some time.'

Guilt clenched at him. While he'd been stewing about the way she'd walked away, right when things seemed to have been going so fine, he'd greedily forgotten why he was really there. He'd promised to watch her back. He'd already let her down. Some white knight he was.

'We've monopolised her terribly,' Virginia said, blinking at him coquettishly over a glass of champagne—clearly not her first.

Through clenched teeth Hannah said, 'Virginia's been telling Roger all about my lack of flair for any of the Young Tasmanian pageant sections she aced as a kid.'

'Has she, now?' Bradley asked, frowning at Virginia. It didn't make a dent.

It seemed it would take more than his presence to give Hannah the upper hand. All he could think of for her to do was the same thing he'd done in order to shake off the shackles of his own mother's disappointment. Prove to her, himself and the world that it didn't matter.

'On that note,' he said, 'did you forget we're up next?'

'Up?'

'Karaoke.'

'But I thought you couldn't sing,' Roger said.

'I can't,' Hannah said, hand to her heart, eyes all but popping from her head.

'She's not kidding. She really can't.' That was Virginia.

Having seen enough, he reached in, took Hannah by the hand and dragged her from the local axis of evil. He shot them a little over-the-shoulder wave before he took their plaything away.

He skirted his way through the crowd in silence. Hannah

kept close, tucking in behind him when things became overly cramped. Her small hand in his felt good. Really good.

'Maid of honour business all finished?' he asked, his voice gruff.

'It is, thank you,' she said stiffly. 'Now where are you taking me?'

'I said we were going to sing, so now we have to sing.'

Suddenly his arm was almost yanked from its socket. He spun to find she'd dug in her heels and was refusing to budge.

He glanced towards the cocktail lounge. 'It we don't they'll just think it was a dodgy excuse for you to ditch them.'

'Wasn't it?'

'Only if you're happy with them thinking so.'

Two little frown lines appeared above her nose, and she nibbled at her full lower lip. He found himself staring. Imagining. Planning.

Finally she shook her head. 'But I really can't sing.'

'Can *they*?' He motioned to the wannabe boy band who could barely slur out a sentence yet still had a rapt and voluble audience. 'Now, pick a song. Something you can recite in your sleep.'

'Oh, God. This is really happening, isn't it? Umm... In my dreams when I audition for random TV talent shows I'm always singing something from *Grease*.'

He felt a grin coming at the thought of such innocent dreams, and struggled to bite it back.

Apparently not well enough. Her face fell. 'You don't know *Grease*, do you? Well, I am *not* going up there on my own.'

'You're safe. I had the biggest crush on Olivia Newton-John when I was a kid.'

The manic tugging relaxed instantly as she gawped at him. He used her moment of distraction to drag her to the edge of the stage.

'I love it!' she said, grinning from ear to ear. 'You used to sing her songs into your mum's hairbrush, didn't you? You can tell me. I promise I won't tell a soul. Well, bar Sonja, of course—and you know how discreet *she* is.'

She shook her head, her thick dark hair curling over her shoulders—sexy, unbridled, exposing a curve of soft golden skin just below her right ear that was crying out for a set of teeth to sink into it.

He stared at the spot, finding himself wholly distracted by the imagined taste of her spilling into his mouth. Better that than to brood over the fact that somehow he'd promised to leap onto a spotlit stage and in the act of performing beg a crowd of strangers for their superficial devotion.

He took solace in Hannah's luscious creamy shoulder as he pulled her closer—close enough to lose himself in the last subtle trails of her scent as he whispered in her ear, 'What the lady wants, the lady gets. *Grease* it is.'

Then he turned her in his arms and pointed to the stage, looming dark and high in front of them.

Her smile disappeared and she swallowed hard. 'So we're really doing this?'

'One song. Show them that even though you have no flair for pageantry you have pluck to spare.'

'You think I have pluck?'

He turned away from the stage at the softness in her voice, only to find himself drowning in the heat of her eyes. 'To spare.'

She blinked at him. Long dark lashes stroked her cheek, creating flutters as he imagined their light graze caressing his skin as she kissed her way up his—

She breathed deep and shook out her hands. 'Let's do it. Now. Quick. Before I change my mind.'

He went to move away and she grabbed his hand again. Hers was warm, soft, small—and shaking. Trusting.

Holding on tight, he had a quick word in the ear of the guy in charge of the karaoke line-up, and slipped him a twenty so that they could get this over and done with as soon as humanly possible.

'Okay,' she said, bouncing from foot to foot, tipping her head from side to side to ease her neck. Warming up as if she was about to do a triple-jump, not a little show tune. 'We've established that I'm doing this because I'm a cowardly pleaser. But why are *you*?'

'When in Rome…'

She shook her head. 'I've worked right by your side for nearly a year now, Bradley. I know you. Putting yourself up there like some piece of meat to be picked over must be akin to torture.'

She was so close to the truth—a truth he had no intention of sharing with her or anyone—he shut his mouth and avoided those big, clear, candid eyes.

'Fine,' she said. 'Don't tell me. I'll figure it out eventually.'

And then she smiled. The smile of a woman who knew him. Who cared enough to *try* to know him. A woman who didn't care if he knew it too.

Dammit. He was in the middle of a bar without a drink, and if he'd ever needed Dutch courage the time was now.

Lucky for her the thing propelling him forward was his inability to stand by and allow her to be so summarily dismissed. He'd rewritten his story. He wasn't merely a little orphan boy any more. He was a man who conquered mountains and showed others how to do the same.

What Hannah had yet to realise was that in going up on that stage it wouldn't matter if she proved her mother right by not holding a tune. What would matter was that her story would no longer be about being her mother's great disappointment. Her story would be the time she summoned the kind of guts she never knew she had in order to belt out a song at her sister's fabulous pre-wedding party.

And, in the spirit of watching her back, if he had to endure a little excruciating drama to give that to her, then so be it.

The current song had stopped. The guys were ushered off-stage to a round of bawdy cheers.

Bradley took Hannah's hand and dragged her limp body on-stage. Once there, he gave her a little push till she was beneath the glare of the spotlight. And, just as he'd hoped, the second they saw who was on stage the crowd cheered like nobody's business.

She laughed softly. And blushed. Then curtsied. The crowd went wild.

Her face glistened with perspiration. Her eyes were wild and glittering. But her chin jutted forward, as if she was daring *anyone* to tell her this was something she couldn't do. The strength of her inner steel surprised him. It even seemed to steady him until he stared, undaunted, out through the bright lights to the braying faceless crowd beyond.

The strains of 'You're the One That I Want' blared from the speakers, and the entire club got to its feet and cheered as one.

Hannah came to, as if from a trance, lowered her microphone, and looked up into his eyes. 'Can *you* sing?'

He put the mike back to her lips and said, 'We're certainly about to find out.'

Hannah's high heels dangled from one hand as she padded across the marble floor towards the bank of lifts leading to the Gatehouse's extensive rooms.

Her ears rang from the after-effects of hours of overly loud music, while her limbs felt loose and languid. The rest of her buzzed from a mix of cocktails and exhaustion and coming down from the high of her karaoke duet with Bradley which had brought the house down.

She turned to walk backwards, smiling at her partner in crime who strolled along behind her. 'Of all the crazy moments of this bizarre night, the biggest shock has to be the fact that you can really sing!'

'So you've mentioned once or twice,' he drawled, his eyes following her closely as she swayed.

'I suck. I mean, I *really* suck. But you were right—it didn't matter. I felt like a rock star. And, no matter how strong and silent you are being about the issue, I know that somehow you knew I would.'

'Lucky guess,' he said, quietly eating up the distance between them.

She grimaced at her bare feet, indecision warring with the most intense sexual attraction she'd ever felt. Judging by the tumble of sensations bombarding her every sense as her eyes met his, it was clear which was winning.

Needing some physical distance from all that manly heat, she skipped over to the lift and pressed the 'up' button. In the quiet, deserted foyer it made such a loud noise she giggled. 'Shhh!'

'Shhh, yourself.'

'Nah,' she said, nice and loud. 'No shushing me tonight. I have sung in front of strangers and friends alike, I have sung badly, and yet I have survived. That calls for a lack of shushing. It calls for dancing.'

So she danced. Her bare feet sticking to the floor, her hips swaying, her arms flying out sideways, she started spinning and spinning and spinning. She'd been so scared of being judged and found wanting for so long she'd only done things she knew she was great at. And she'd done them as well as she humanly could.

Now, having thrown herself at something that had always been tied up in her mind with a deep-down bruising kind of hurt, she realised it wasn't so scary after all. She felt as if she could do anything. Fly. Play the ukulele. Bradley...

When his strong, solid arm slid around her waist—when he pulled her close and began to sway to the beat of the tune inside his head—she wondered if her desire had been so immense she'd summoned him to her against his will.

Then again, there was nothing forced about the way his body pressed against hers, the way his chin rested atop her head, the way his hand cradled her waist. Nothing mistakable about the hard jut she felt pressed into her belly.

He spun her out and tugged her back in. Giddy laughter shot from her lungs as she tried to regain her footing. When he tucked her tight into the warm cocoon of his embrace he was humming. Something slow and soft and sweet and poignant, melodic and unrecognisable. And quieting.

She leant her droopy head on his shoulder—or as close as she could get since it was so very, very high off the ground and she was barefoot on tippy-toes. In fact she was closer to his heart. She could feel the steady beat against her cheek. It was the very same beat that throbbed within her.

He did better. He lifted her till her feet were on top of his.

What could she do but throw her shoes over her shoulder and thread her hands around his neck, slide her fingers through the springy thick hair at the back of his neck? How long had it been since she'd first ached to do just that?

And now she was slow-dancing.

With Bradley.

With her boss.

Somewhere deep down inside her a little voice tried reminding her why that was a bad idea. She shook her head to shut it up. Didn't it realise that she couldn't remember ever, in her whole life, feeling this way? As if she was made of melted marshmallow, all hot and soft and sweet and yummy.

She breathed in deep and was soon drowning in the heavenly scent of hot, clean, male skin. No man in the world had ever smelled so good. So sexy. So edible.

The lift doors opened with a loud 'bing'. Neither of them paid it any heed.

Hannah pulled her head away from its heavenly pillow and looked up into the most beautiful mercury-grey eyes on the planet.

She threaded her fingers deeper into Bradley's hair, her thumb caressing the soft spot beneath his ear. His eyes grew dark, like the sky before a winter storm.

The swaying stopped. He pulled her tighter still, and the air escaped her lungs as her head rocked back on her all but useless neck. Moonlight slanted across his strong, angular profile as though all it wanted was to touch him too.

So big, she thought, *so tall. So private. So exceptional. So, so beautiful.*

Bradley lifted her off his feet and placed her gently on the floor. The marble beneath her bare feet was ice-cold, but the rest of her was filled with a licking flame so hot it barely registered.

Neither did the lift doors as they slowly slid closed.

And then, as though it was the most natural thing in the world, Bradley bent his head and kissed her.

Hannah's eyes fluttered closed as fireworks exploded behind her eyes, and then down and down and down her body, until she felt as if her blood was made of popping bubbles.

He pulled back, his lips hovering millimetres from hers. Giving her the chance to stop things before they went any further. But it was way too late. The kiss was out there. For eternity. There was no going back now.

Whether it was because of the press of her hips to his, or the miserable groan that rumbled through her, he held back no more.

He slid his hand deep into her hair and his mouth plundered hers until she could barely breathe for the intensity of feeling cascading through her.

When his tongue slid knowingly across hers that was the absolute end of her. She was gone—lost in a swirl of sensation and heat and need. She lifted up onto her toes and wrapped her arms around his neck, pressing as close as she could. Needing to feel his warmth, his skin, his realness. Aflame with the impossible desire to crawl inside him.

But in her bare feet he was too tall, too big, too far away, and she wanted to be closer. She wanted to be a part of him.

Buoyed by frustration and desire for the liberating sense of release she leapt into his arms, wrapping her legs about his hips.

His hands cupped her, holding her as if she weighed nothing. But his kiss deepened, heated, ratcheted up a dozen levels—as if she meant anything *but* nothing to him. As if his own long-held frustration had broken through a dam and now nothing was going to stop it.

And then his lips were on her neck, her collarbone, her bare shoulder. His teeth sank into the tendon below her neck and she cried out in pleasure, her hands gripping the back of his head. The most delicious heat she had ever known pooled deep inside her.

She sighed and murmured, 'If I'd had a clue this would feel *this* good I'd never have been able to hold back all these months.'

Hannah felt Bradley stiffen in her arms. Then the lift went *bing*. Or maybe it happened the other way around.

Either way, the sound of the lift opening registered somewhere in the fuzz that was Hannah's brain at about the same time she felt Bradley's arms unwinding from around her.

She looked into his eyes, confusion taking hold of her still liquefied system. But she didn't have time to decipher a thing as a pile of Elyse's friends spilled out of the lift, laughing, screaming, half way to being drunk.

She scrambled to fix her hair. Her lipstick. Her crumpled clothes. Then saw her discarded shoes were in their stumbling path. She leapt away from Bradley, grabbed the shoes out of their way before somebody impaled themselves on a stiletto.

'Hannah Banana!' one of Elyse's oldest friends called out, grabbing her and trying to pull her in their wake. She managed to extricate herself and tell them to have fun. And then, as suddenly as they'd appeared, there was nothing left of them but their echoing laughter.

The quiet foyer was filled with nothing but the sound of her puffing breaths. Adrenalin poured through her like a flood, till her body shook from the shock. Her body—which was still throbbing from head to toe as it baked in the intensity of Bradley's kiss.

Bradley.

Shoes gripped in her tight fist, she glanced up to find him watching her. A huge dark shadow of a figure in the pale moonlight. Hands in pockets. Still as a mountain.

The lift 'binged' again. This time instinct had her stepping inside. The doors started to close until she reached out and held them at bay.

'Coming up?' she asked, shoes swinging against her leg.

A muscle worked in his jaw as he flicked a glance up in the direction of their suite. Then he took a step back. 'You go. I'm going to track down a nightcap.'

The fact that they had a crazily well-stocked bar in their über-suite seemed to have eluded him. Or perhaps not. Hannah felt a wretched little cramp in her stomach. She wished Elyse's friends would return, so she could throttle them one by one.

'Okay,' she sing-songed, as though she didn't realise she'd just been wholeheartedly rejected. Then, falling back into ever helpful assistant mode, she said, 'I'm pretty sure the foyer bar is open all night.'

He nodded. Yet didn't move.

The cramp in her stomach gave way to hope. Maybe he was being a gentleman, waiting for a sign from her. Though she wasn't sure she knew a bigger sign than throwing herself into a guy's arms and wrapping her thighs around him.

The lift 'binged' several times, ready to get a move on. She clenched her teeth and jabbed at the 'open door' button till it shut the hell up. Didn't it realise what a delicate moment this was?

Maybe that was the problem. Maybe subtlety didn't work on mountains. Maybe the guy needed not a sign but a sledgehammer.

'Bradley, would you like to—?'

'Get some sleep.' He cut her off. 'It's been a big day.'

Her stomach sank like a stone dropped into the lake behind their hotel. She desperately tried to locate some dormant thread of sophistication somewhere inside her but just ended up babbling. 'Right. Sleep. What a great idea. Just what I need.'

Clearly to him what had just happened was just a kiss. And a little necking. And, okay, some extremely dextrous fondling. Maybe it was an everyday occurrence for him and it had simply been her turn. Maybe she'd come on too strong and he already regretted it. Maybe. But then again he'd absolutely come on to her first.

As her head began to spin, the only thing Hannah knew was that she should take his advice and get the hell out of there before she said or did something really stupid.

She looked away to jab hard and fast at the number for their floor. 'Goodnight, Bradley.'

He nodded. 'I'll see you in the morning.'

Slowly, slowly the lift door closed. When her own reflection stared back at her and the lift began to rumble she could still see his face clear as day. Dark. Stormy. Stoic.

Somehow, some way, whatever forces had come together to create that moment back there had disappeared as if in a puff of smoke. If only she knew why.

CHAPTER SEVEN

BRADLEY cradled the now lukewarm cup of coffee in his palms as he sat in the big, empty foyer bar.

Unfortunately the mind-numbing normality of a late-night coffee hadn't done a damn thing to numb one bit of him.

He wasn't a reckless man. Even as he'd lowered his head to kiss Hannah's soft, pink smiling lips he'd known there would be consequences. He'd weighed them, measured them, and decided that after negotiating such a riotous night with commendable finesse a celebratory kiss was a pretty fine idea.

What he hadn't expected was for the effortless sensuality she wore so lightly to explode into a raging furnace the second his lips had touched hers. Though that he could handle.

What had him sitting alone in a bar at three in the morning was, *'If I'd had a clue this would feel this good I'd never have been able to hold back all those months.'*

Her words hadn't stopped ringing inside his head since he'd sat down.

It appeared as though Hannah had feelings for him. Perhaps only nascent ones, but that was still too much. He'd never let himself become involved with any woman who didn't view relationships with the same lack of gravity he did. Doing so would be nothing short of hypocritical. He knew all too well how it felt to have the world you thought you knew cut out from under you.

So why did the same mouth that back-chatted constantly,

barked remonstrations whenever he ran late, and grinned delightedly any time he was pushed outside of his comfort zone have to be an instant gateway to paradise?

Dammit. He pushed the porcelain cup aside in frustration.

'Another, Mr Knight?' the barman asked.

'No thanks, mate,' he said, his voice ragged. 'I think I've done enough damage for the night.'

'Very good, sir.'

Bradley hauled his heavy self from the bar stool and walked slowly to the lift. Standing on the very spot where for the sake of that mouth he'd ignored the signs and kissed her anyway.

The lift door opened and he stepped inside. He looked at his feet rather than his reflection in the mirrored doors, not wanting to look himself in the eye as he considered things again.

Hannah liked him. He'd never use that to his advantage. If he did he'd be no better than those who'd hurt him in the pursuit of making their own lives a tad more comfortable.

Even though she kissed like a siren. As if there was a fountain of untapped heat bubbling beneath her small frame. As if she wanted nothing more than for *him* to be the one to release it.

All he could hope was that by the time he got back to their shared suite Hannah's room would be dark and quiet. Then he could retire to his own room, strip down, open his bedroom window as wide as it would go and let lashings of bitterly ice-cold air do what will-power and boiling hot coffee could not.

Bradley shut the suite door behind him as quietly as humanly possible. Ears pricked, he couldn't hear anything beyond the faint swoosh of winter wind gently buffeting the unadorned windows that stretched the entire length of the shared living space.

He shucked off his shoes and lifted a foot to sneak to his room. Then he heard a noise. His whole body clenched and adrenalin kicked his senses into overdrive.

He heard it again. It sounded like the clink of glass on wood. Probably a tree branch scraping against the window. Only one way to be sure.

He padded down the wide steps into the lounge, to find all the lights were off bar a lamp at one end of the modern cream leather four-seater couch. Beneath the lamp a magazine was open and turned face-down. In the far corner of the room embers burned red in the fireplace. It seemed Hannah hadn't been able to instantly fall into the sleep of the innocent either.

The clink pinged in his ears again and he turned towards the sound. It was coming from the corner of the room in which the spa pool sat, tucked into an alcove with a window over-looking the forest. It was hidden discreetly from view behind a half-wall.

Blood pumping in his ears, Bradley took two more steps. The deep dark blue of a large square dipping pool came slowly into view...

And there she was.

Hannah. Awake. Sitting on the edge of the pool. Top half covered in a loose pale grey sweater. Naked legs dangling into the lapping water. A half-glass of red wine at her fingers. A hot pink cowboy hat sitting incongruously atop her head.

The groan he swallowed down was deep and painful. For she couldn't have looked any sexier if she'd tried.

He could walk away right now and pretend he'd never seen her. *Pretend to who?* a strangled voice shouted inside his head. *Because sure as you're a grown man you ain't ever going to forget it!*

Her fingers reached out and played with the stem of the glass, twirling it back and forth. The edge of her top slipped, revealing the creamy skin of one beautiful bare shoulder.

Skin he'd tasted less than an hour before. Skin that tasted of honey and heat and such sweetness he couldn't get it out of his head.

He took a step closer.

She turned her head. He stopped, the toes of his right foot clamping together as he held himself statue-still. But she only looked as far as her glass, her long hair shielding half her face like a curtain of brown silk. She dipped a finger into the glass and brought it to her lips, slowly sucking the red droplet into her mouth.

Something finally alerted her to his presence—probably the fact that his blood was pumping so hard and fast through his body people could hear it three floors down—and she turned with a fright, her hand to her chest.

'Where did you spring from?' she asked, breathless.

'The bar,' he said, sounding as if he'd swallowed a ream of sandpaper. 'Had a coffee. They do pretty good coffee. Now I'm back.'

Bradley Knight, the great communicator.

'What's the time?' She glanced at her huge watch, her eyes opening wide as she saw how long had passed since they'd parted.

'It's late,' he agreed. But he didn't give a hoot. It might as well have been ten in the morning. He felt so alert. So conscious of every sound, every movement, every shift and sway of her nubile half-naked form. 'What's with the hat?'

'The—? Oh.' Her eyes practically crossed as she looked up. 'You wanted to know what was in my suitcase? This. And feather boas. A hot pink veil. Dozens of packets of condoms. A box of dried rose petals. A veritable traveling maid-of-honour's just-in-case bag of tricks.'

She took off the hat, strands of her dark hair catching in the weave. She ran her fingers through the waves till they fell in messy kinks across her shoulders.

His feet moved as though driven by a deeper force.

'Couldn't sleep?' he asked.

She twirled the hat around one finger and caught it before it tipped into the pool. 'Wasn't entirely sure I wanted to.'

She shot him a quick glance. Far too quick for him to be able to read it fully. But the fact that she was up, waiting... It would be rude not to join her.

'Perhaps that's because we never did get to finish that dance,' he rumbled, hating himself even as he said it. If he was Catholic he'd be spinning Hail Marys in his head. As it was he was pretty sure he was going straight to hell.

'Mmm,' she said. 'We were rudely interrupted before the big finale.'

'It did feel like we were building up to...something.'

She raised an eyebrow. 'I was all prepared for a grand Hollywood dip. You?'

Despite the tension swirling about the room, Bradley laughed.

She laughed too, her cheeks pinkening charmingly. She pulled her knees up to her chin. Water glistened down her lean pale gold legs. Toenails painted every colour of the rainbow twinkled in the misty light reflecting back off the water. She had been busy while he was away. And he didn't blame her. If she felt anything like he did she'd have to climb a mountain to have any chance at burning off the adrenalin rocketing through her system.

Damn, but she was something. Sexy, playful, smart, and completely unpretentious. And in his world—a world peopled by pretenders—that was a truly unique quality. All this from a woman who, somewhere in her room, had dozens of packets of just-in-case condoms. Just sitting there. Going to waste.

She watched out of the corner of her eye as he slowly rolled up the legs of his jeans. She rubbed her chin on her shoulder, her eyes straying over the flecks of hair covering his mountaineer's calves.

In two steps he was beside her, sinking down onto the cool

tiles, his bare feet all but sighing in pleasure as they dipped into the glistening hot water. The temperature came close to matching the heat his body was already radiating now he was sitting within touching distance of that shoulder, that hair, those legs. That mouth.

It was all there for the taking. If only her expectations weren't too high. Or his too low. If only they could meet somewhere…

'I have a proposal,' Bradley said, before he even felt the words coming.

She blinked at him. 'Do you, now?'

'I do. And here it is. You're here another three days. I have nowhere else to be. And this suite is built for all the decadence and debauchery a wild weekend can muster.'

Her chest rose and fell as she breathed deep. But she didn't for a moment look away.

'I propose we don't waste another minute. But here's the clincher. Come Tuesday…whatever happens in Tasmania stays in Tasmania.'

Her hands curled over the tiled edge of the spa pool until the knuckles turned white. His did the same. He moved his finger half an inch and it connected with hers. Her head dropped back and a tremble shook through her.

And in the end that was all it took. An arrangement they could both live with and the touch of a finger.

With a moan that was half-anguish and half-relief Hannah straddled him in one deft move. Her hands were deep in his hair, her mouth on his, and she was kissing him as though her life depended on it.

That mouth. It was nothing short of divine. Bradley wrapped his arms about her oh-so-slight form, closed his eyes, and let that gorgeous mouth take him to heaven and back. Deal or no deal, that mouth was as close to heaven as he was ever likely to get.

Eons later the kisses slowed. Softened. Sweetened. His

hormones continued to rage through him, looking for release. Gentle discovery was such gorgeous agony.

Hands on his shoulders, she kissed his temple. His cheek. The very corner of his mouth. He turned to take sanctuary there again, but she moved on to nibble at his earlobe.

'Devil,' he groaned.

Her laughter whispered across his ear, soft and sexy. Just like her.

He slid his hands straight to her backside and pulled her close, dragging the curve between her thighs across the hard peak of his denim-clad erection. She gasped and clung to him, her teasing laughter nothing but a memory.

He registered a pair of underpants before his hands slipped beneath her top. His thumbs ran over her hipbones, his fingers delving into the soft, feminine flesh at her waist. His exploration continued and he found nothing but skin. Scorching hot, velvet-soft naked skin.

When his thumbs brushed the underside of her bare breasts she bucked in pleasure. His stomach clenched tight to keep himself upright. To keep him from knocking himself out on the tiles or falling into the spa.

Though the thought of Hannah slippery and wet was almost enough to blow his mind, the thought of being stuck in wet jeans and unable to shuck his way out of the blasted things kept him rooted to the spot.

He cupped her breast to find a perfect handful. Beautiful. Every inch of her was staggeringly beautiful. The way she reacted at his slightest touch overwhelmed him again and again. He knew he had skills. But Hannah made him feel like a Grand Master. It only made him want to prove her right. To prove to them both their pact would be worth it.

But before he even had the chance she'd whipped her top over her head. Then, with a twinkle in her eye, she was gone. The warm body writhing so deliciously in his arms was now nothing but a cool empty space.

It took him a moment to realise Hannah had slipped into the spa. Then she reappeared, water streaming over her face, glistening from her long dark hair. Hot, wet, slippery. And then a tiny pair of black underpants appeared on a twirling finger before she flipped them onto the tiles.

Bradley was on his feet, stripping down before he even realised what was happening. Jacket. Top. Singlet. Jeans.

Dammit. Button fly!

His fingers felt fat and numb as he struggled with what felt like a thousand buttons.

He slipped into the water, searching for her. The damn pool wasn't any more than two metres by two metres, but the floor was a mottled midnight-blue, and lit only by the filmiest of winter moonlight.

Then he felt the slightest pressure on his inner thigh. His hipbone. His belly button. It was her lips as she kissed her way up his body.

She emerged from the water like some kind of siren. Dark slick hair, skin like cream, mouth creating the most delicious havoc with his senses.

He leaned his elbows on the tiles, relishing the cold hardness, hoping it might keep him from teetering over the edge into oblivion. It did. Barely.

She slid a slow hand up his chest. Her tongue followed, creating a burning hot path across his ribs, around his left nipple. Her soft naked flesh slid sensually against his.

And then, as her teeth sank hard into the sensitive tendon across the top of his shoulder, her other hand wrapped around his erection. One finger at a time. Till she had him in her complete thrall.

The primal growl building up inside him finally found release. It echoed against the black windows. It reverberated across the top of the water. And Hannah's grip, both up top and below, faltered.

At the first sign of a pause in her utterly sensual seduction of him he wrested back control.

He lifted her out of the pool, spun her about, and sat her unceremoniously on the tiles.

She squeaked in shock, her limbs flailing as she tried to get purchase on the slippery floor. She sat before him completely naked, nowhere to hide.

She looked down at him. Wide pale eyes rimmed by smudged eyeliner. Pink-peaked breasts turning to dark nubs in the cooler air.

Vulnerable. Completely at his mercy. He realised with a jolt what kind of responsibility that engendered. Just what kind of line he was treading.

Then her naked foot slid up his side. He jerked beneath the heated caress. Shuddered. Then focussed. She was a grown woman. A woman who knew the boundaries. A woman who wanted this as much as he did.

Bradley placed his hands on her knees. She flinched. *Good*, he thought. He wanted her completely aware of what was about to happen to her.

She never looked away. When he began to press them apart slowly, oh-so-achingly slowly, she let him.

Her eyes grew dark—so unexpectedly dark, so beautifully dark. Her lips parted. Her skin grew pink. All over. How had he never noticed the sensuality that oozed from her pores?

Fine. He'd noticed. He'd just worked the both of them to the point of exhaustion every time his body reacted to her, in an effort to keep his life uncomplicated.

Fool.

He yanked her closer, her backside sliding along the tiles till her legs dangled in the water. A surprised sigh rushed from her lungs. Then he lifted her legs slowly, one by one, and draped them over his shoulders. Her heels bounced against his back, creating hot swirls of need that coiled tightly in his gut. And while a thousand conflicting emotions flittered across her face she gave in to him without a murmur. Loose as a rag doll, she slowly lay back on the tiles, her head coming to rest on his rolled-up jacket.

Trusting him completely.

Again realisation jarred him. How could she? Why would she? He'd never done anything to engender such faith from her. He was pretty hard guy most of the time, and she didn't seem to care. She needed to toughen up. Big-time. And fast.

He'd tell her so. Later. Much later. For right then all his brain function went into demanding that his hand run down her front, graze her breasts, take its time over the sexy little rise at her belly. Her torso lifted and curled to follow the trail of his touch, as if not being touched by him was simply too much to bear.

Desire the likes of which he'd never felt roared unimpeded through him, lit by a need to please her. To show her that her trust wasn't unfounded. And to drive every thought she'd ever had completely out of her mind.

Then he lowered his mouth to her inner thigh, the scent of her making his nostrils flare in anticipation. Her hands slammed out sideways, grabbing onto his shirt, his jeans, whatever purchase she could find.

He ran his tongue along the muscle quivering in her thigh. God, she was temptation incarnate. So responsive, so lush. How he managed to keep from hauling her back into the water and having his way with her he had no idea.

He pressed her legs further apart again. Her heels dug into his back, tugging him closer. Her desire for him was so bold he ached. A gorgeous, pleading little whimper escaped that beautiful mouth, and he lowered his own mouth to the warm waiting juncture.

He took her to the very edge of madness, and himself right along with her. She endured and endured and endured the pleasure with rabid delight—until she finally hit a height of pleasure even she could no longer maintain and completely fell apart.

He kept his hands on her, feeding off her luxuriation as a series of aftershocks trembled through her. The way she responded was so gratifying he could have done the same again and again. All night long if she'd let him.

When the trembles abated, he slid his thumbs up her thighs till her hands clamped down on his.

It seemed she had other ideas.

She pulled herself upright, clearly having been sapped of a good deal of her strength. *He'd* done that. It gave him a hell of a buzz to know he'd turned her to jelly.

She slid slowly back into the water. He held her by the waist and helped her. As her feet touched the bottom, she held his face in both hands and looked deep into his eyes. All he could do was breathe and look right back.

No fear. No reticence. No holding back. No regret.

Rules or no rules, boundaries or no boundaries, somewhere inside him a portal opened, so that he felt her serenity, her surety, her blissed-out satisfaction infiltrating him. It was as if he was physically experiencing her afterglow.

Then she smiled. A smile fuelled by pure sin.

Wham! All sense of serenity fled as he was slapped across the face with the triple threat of that inner light. That natural impudence. That glorious mouth.

The portal snapped shut. His erection ached.

His turn had come.

The condoms.

Hell. Hadn't she said they were in her suitcase?

Bradley was so far gone he couldn't even remember which direction her room was. The idea of a mad dash to her room and back was about as appealing as eating fried worms.

But she was on the pill. That little pearl had come up in conversation at some point. Could he let that be enough? God, he wished he could let that be enough—

Hannah reached over, and from next to her discarded wine glass appeared a square foil packet. She *had* been waiting for him. With intent. His divine little siren. He wondered how many of the dozens of packets she'd strewn around the suit, *just in case*. Then again he didn't give a damn. Right now he only needed one.

She peeled the packet from around the latex disk with her teeth. Then slid slowly back into the water, dark, dark eyes looking right into his. She moved up to him, rolled the sheath into place, slowly wrapped her legs around his hips, and lowered herself onto him. He pressed deep, perfectly deep, into her ready flesh, as though he'd been waiting his whole life for that moment.

Twenty-four hours, a small voice reminded him. *Somewhere between twenty-four hours and twelve months.* And he had no more than three days in which to fully satisfy himself.

With that divine mouth gently tugging at his, that heavenly tongue sliding along his, those clever teeth creating havoc with his earlobes, she rode him.

Slowly. Achingly slowly. Then faster. And harder.

He took over, losing himself inside her until the pressure became too much. Too wild. Too heavy. Too powerful. And he came as he'd never come before.

He could feel her playing with the back of his hair. Her chin rested lightly on his shoulder, her outward breaths puffed against his earlobe.

All that heat and release and temptation and response, from the light, lean creature bobbing in his arms.

Compared with the intensity of what they'd just experienced she felt so slight. So small. So breakable. He felt an immense urge to hold her close. To keep her safe from all harm.

It was a crazy thought. Random. And impossible. Especially considering *he* was the biggest threat she had in her line of sight right then.

He slowly uncurled her from around him, hoping physical

distance might make the floor of the spa not feel as if it was about to give way at any moment.

Only the second she lifted her head and smiled up at him, all lethargy and loose limbs, his gaze went straight to her mouth. To her moist pink lips. Between one breath and the next his body revved up like a hot-rod car, waiting for the green light. And all he could think was, *More*.

Apprehension flashed inside his head. If *that* hadn't sated him, at least for the moment, what on earth would it take? Well, whatever it took, it had to be done by the end of the long weekend.

It was already after four in the morning on day two. They had hours of daylight in which to sleep. It certainly wouldn't hurt him taking until sunrise to find out *just* what it might take to get Hannah Gillespie out of his system for good.

With a caveman grunt, he hauled her over his shoulder and walked them out of the pool.

'Where do you think you're taking me?' she yelled, laughing, pounding useless hands on his back.

'Bed.'

She lifted her head and tried to angle it around to see his face. Her backside wriggled against his cheek. He literally began to shake with arousal. Sunrise was an arbitrary end point, surely?

'Bed?' she cried. 'But we're sopping wet!'

'That's why I'm going to yours,' he added.

She laughed. Easy, free, gorgeous. Ready for more. Ready for anything.

He kicked open her bedroom door. This was going to be some night.

Waves of gold and pink blurred across the backs of Hannah's eyelids. Keeping her eyes closed, she stretched, her naked limbs sliding unhindered across her massive bed.

She creaked her eyes open to find sunlight pouring through

the windows. It was morning. Make that late morning. And muscles she hadn't even known existed twinged in protest.

Then, in a rush of bright and beautiful heat, it all came back to her.

Bradley. The slow dance. The kiss. The rebuff. The resolution not to take it lying down, so to speak. The spa. Oh, my—the spa! And lastly, but certainly not least of all, hours and hours of the most intense feats of sexual prowess in the bed in which she now lay.

Taking a sheet with her, she curled luxuriously onto her side. And grinned.

'Wow,' she whispered, her voice rough and husky.

Wow, indeed. If anyone had asked how she'd hoped the first day of her long-awaited holiday might turn out, she'd never, even in her wildest dreams, have imagined she'd end up in bed with the boss.

A whisper of cool air tickled at her feet. And at her conscience. She curled up tighter and rubbed them together.

Everything was fine. Gorgeous, even. Had been from the moment Bradley had opened his beautiful mouth and said the magic words, *'Whatever happens in Tasmania stays in Tasmania.'*

The second he'd uttered those words the fantasies that had niggled at the corner of her mind since she'd known him had been given free rein. Within limits. Limits that meant she had no choice but to put a stop to any hope this might become more. Limits that gave her the comfort that in the aftermath Bradley wanted things to go back to normal too.

And once they got back to town—to real life, to work— they could both count on the fact that everything that had happened that weekend would be over. Niggling desires satisfied. Blissfully, beautifully, erotically satisfied.

Bradley could go back to being aloof and cool and stubborn and untouchable.

And she could happily continue…

What? Not dating? Ignoring the sensual side of herself so as to concentrate on her serious side? While hoping to one day magically find herself a man who could give her the love and loyalty and romance and openness that she refused to settle without? A man who would somehow manage to live up to what had happened to her last night. Who could make her feel wanton and cherished and beautiful and sexual, as she did when Bradley's lips were on hers. When his teeth scraped over her hipbone. When his tongue slid around her breast. So far, in the first twenty-five years of her life, she'd never even come close to feeling that way with any other man.

Hell.

The crackle of oil popping on a frying pan sizzled through the ajar door. Breakfast! The desire to stick her head under the pillow and stay there for ever had to wait. It turned out she was beyond hungry. Stomach-rumblingly, mind-numbingly famished. And the man of the moment had ordered Room Service.

She wrapped a massive king-sized sheet around herself, and made a quick stop to check herself in the bathroom mirror.

'Wow,' she said again.

Her eyes were huge wells of liquid green, surrounded by smudges of leftover make-up. Her lips were puffy. Her cheeks pink and warm. She looked ruffled, tousled, and well-ravaged.

She glanced towards the door. Well, he was the one who'd done that too her. And brilliantly too. What was the point of pretending nothing had happened when it most certainly had? Without fixing a hair on her head, she swept up her makeshift toga and headed towards the delicious smell.

Halfway to the über-modern, stainless steel and Caesar stone kitchenette, Hannah pulled up short.

Bradley was cooking. And he was cooking what looked and smelled a heck of a lot like eggs Benedict with extra bacon.

Her favourite meal on the entire planet. She was ninety-nine percent sure she'd told him as much. A few dozen times.

He'd remembered. Just as he'd remembered her favourite drink. While seeming intent on nothing more than working her to the bone, he'd paid attention. Her stomach felt as if it had been inhabited by a chorus line doing fan kicks.

He looked up, his quicksilver eyes grazing her naked shoulders before moving down the massive expanse of white sheet trailing behind her. It felt as if his hands had followed the same path.

'Good morning,' he said.

'Oh, so it *is* still morning?'

'Just.'

'How long have you been up?'

'A while.' He glanced at the empty coffee cup and open newspaper on the glass-topped breakfast table.

With a yawn, and an inelegant hitch of her sheet, she said, 'You should have woken me.'

His mouth hooked into the kind of half-smile that made the chorus line in her stomach start bumping into one another in blissful confusion.

'I could have,' he said. 'But I thought you might need the rest.' He didn't need to add, *After last night's marathon efforts.*

'I'm fine,' she said. Unfortunately another yawn cut off her declaration halfway through.

Bradley laughed softly, then turned away as a pair of English muffin-halves popped up from a toaster.

Hannah and her sheet managed to curl up on a gilded, beautifully adorned, wrought-iron dining chair. 'This place does have Room Service, you know.'

'Where do you think I got the eggs and muffins?'

'Good point. So, it appears as if the man can cook.' *And sing. And dance. And create amazing television that changes people's lives. And make love like no man I've ever known.*

A warm glow began to fill her. A glow the likes of which she'd never felt before, but her deepest feminine instincts understood all too well. She pulled her sheet tighter in an effort to suffocate it, to forcibly remind herself: *what happens in Tassie stays in Tassie.*

That's your only lifeline here, hon. Hang on tight!

Bradley said, 'A person can't survive on café food and Chinese takeaway alone.'

Hannah flicked the newspaper before closing it. She could beg to differ.

'I am a single man,' Bradley continued, 'living alone. It was learn to cook or starve. You don't cook?'

She shook her head.

'So Sonja cooks?'

Hannah laughed so hard she all but pulled a muscle.

'What do you live on?' he asked.

'Fresh air, hard work, and as many eggs Benedict with extra bacon as I can stomach.'

He laughed again—only this time a small frown creased his forehead. As if he was trying to figure her out. Really trying. She couldn't remember her boss ever doing anything but taking her at face value. The glow inside her began to pulse.

It didn't help that every few seconds images kept springing unbidden into her head. The sensation of hot water lapping against her thrumming naked body as she watched Bradley strip. His mouth becoming more intimate with parts of her than she had herself. The feel of all that hot muscle bunching under her fingernails as she bucked beneath him...

'So, what's the plan for today?'

Bradley's voice cut into her daydreams. She glanced at her wrist, and then rubbed at the naked spot. She must have put her dad's watch somewhere during the night.

'Today's grand plan? Well, I'm sorry to say we missed the practice releasing of the doves. But no matter. Just after lunch there's a sewing class for the girls. And burping contests for the boys.'

She contemplated adding something that involved the entire wedding party getting together to decorate the chapel. But he *was* making her breakfast.

'You *are* kidding?' he said.

'Am I?'

She looked up to find Bradley's eyes had finally contacted fully with hers. Deep, dark, smoky, beautiful grey. Perhaps more distant than they had been hours earlier. But that was forgivable. She was feeling a little tender and unsure herself.

'God, you're easy,' she said. 'There's a day-long movie marathon in the ballroom. Beanbags and blankets to snuggle into as you watch Tim and Elyse's favourite romantic films, one after the other. And this time I'm not kidding.'

His eye twitched at the thought.

'Relax,' she said. 'Since you've been so nice as to make me breakfast, I'm letting you off the hook.'

'Whatever will we do instead?' He licked a blob of hollandaise sauce from his finger, switched off the stove, and moved around the counter. Her body responded like a heat lamp on a chilled lizard—it stretched and unfurled and curved towards the source of heat.

She held on tight to her sheet and put her bare feet flat on the ground. She realised she needed a little time to fully come to terms with what had happened. What was still happening. What Bradley was imagining would happen. At least till Tuesday. And jumping back into bed with Bradley was not going to help.

She held up a hand. 'I have a proposal.'

The last time those words had been spoken between them it had directly led to her pouncing on him. Clearly he remembered it too.

'Do tell.'

She waggled a finger. He stilled. *Good boy.*

'There is a beautiful mountain right on our doorstep. It's a foothill compared with what you're used to, but it's still something really special. There are twenty-odd walking trails, plant and animal varieties found nowhere else on earth, horseback rides, mountain-biking, fly-fishing. Let me show you a sneak peek. If you don't get to see any more of this island than the inside of this hotel, I'll never forgive myself.'

His dark eyes flickered to life, and his mouth curved into the kind of smile that told her that getting to know every inch of the inside of this suite was fine by him.

Her blissfully aching inner thighs tingled in anticipation. But they needed a break. They needed time to recuperate. What better way than an arduous walk around a mountain on a freezing cold morning?

She was going to be the best, most professional tour guide ever.

'Indulge me?' she begged.

'Fine,' he said, finally turning back to the bench where he finished plating up. 'Breakfast first. I need to regain my strength. Then you can be my tour guide. Prove to me why this place makes you go all sentimental and glistening and get that crazy schmaltzy look in your eye.'

Hannah shook her head. 'I'm not sentimental, or a glistener, or in any way schmaltzy. I am a sharp, cool-headed professional.'

He slung a plate in front of her. It smelled insanely good. Soft gooey egg, perfectly toasted muffin, gorgeously rich sauce. She felt herself curling towards it, her nostrils flaring, a hum of appreciation buzzing in her chest. She might even have licked her lips.

'Sharp, cool-headed professional?' he said, grinning at her. 'Want to know the three words *I'd* use to describe you right now?'

She sat up straight. 'No. I really don't.'

Bradley did as he was told and said not another word as he dug into his food.

She did the same. And it tasted as good as it looked. Better, even. Way better. As the egg yolk popped in her mouth and the strong tang of the sauce curled around her tongue she knew it was the best eggs Benedict she'd ever eaten or would likely eat again.

CHAPTER EIGHT

BRADLEY followed the puffs of white from his breath up the steep walking track that took Hannah and himself around the edge of Dove Lake and up into the craggy edges of Cradle Mountain's beautifully eerie crater.

Ice-fresh air burned at his lungs, a clear pale blue sky hovered above, tough and challenging terrain disappeared beneath his feet, and all around was the kind of pristine, unblemished, singular view that climbers and TV audiences alike would go ga-ga over.

This gem of a place had been on the periphery of his life all this time and he'd never even known it was there. Forever in pursuit of the next extreme challenge, he'd never cared to look right under his nose.

Half the thrill had been the fact that he was miles from where he'd come from.

But this felt just as good. It seemed that at some point it had become about new experiences, and not about the exorcism of old ones.

Speaking of new experiences… He felt a tug on the back of his jacket. He turned to find Hannah puffing laboriously behind him.

'Slow…down…please,' she begged, between heaving breaths.

He did as she asked. Her face—or the small part of it he could see in between her beanie hat and the furry neck of the massive parka she'd borrowed from the hotel—was bright pink.

So caught up in his need to burn off some of the adrenalin that still infused him, even after the marathon efforts of that morning, though more likely because of them, he'd forgotten she wasn't an experienced climber herself.

She didn't cook. And by the looks of her she didn't exercise. Two things he'd never known. That, and the fact that she had an adorable strawberry-shaped birthmark in the very centre of her right butt cheek. He wondered what other gems he'd discover about his able assistant this long weekend.

'How much further?' she asked, hands on her knees.

'I thought you were meant to be my tour guide?'

She looked up at him, green eyes sharp. Then she waved a hand around. 'This is Cradle Mountain. That's Dove Lake. Gorgeous, huh? Now can I go back to the hotel?'

He laughed. She glared at him for even being *able* to laugh. It didn't help that she was trying to look angry while dressed in enough clothing for three people. If it wasn't so cold that he couldn't feel his nose, he would have believed she'd gone out of her way *not* to look sexy.

Little did she know he'd spent half the walk intent on getting their little field trip over and done with just so that they could get back to the hotel, where he planned on stripping off those layers one by one.

He glanced ahead. 'Come on. I see somewhere we can stop.'

'Oh, thank God.'

He laughed again. Then moved around behind her to give her a push up the track.

'Now, why didn't I think to wear rollerskates?' she threw over her shoulder. 'You could have done this the whole way.'

'Downhill too?'

'Right. Good point.'

They stepped over the safety fence and took a seat side by side on a large, flat outcrop. Bradley went straight for his water bottle, and jiggled his feet so his muscles wouldn't cramp up. Hannah flopped onto her back and didn't move.

From their position they had a perfect unheeded view over the curving lake and the ragged peaks of once sub-volcanic rock covered in winter green. Spirals of chimney smoke gave away the location of the Gatehouse, otherwise hidden discreetly in the alpine forest.

And if this was a glimpse of what the island had to offer then he was certainly willing to discover more—and soon. Lucky for him he had a human guidebook on the island on his team. One who had indicated an interest in taking a leap forward into producing. He'd half thought she was teasing. Maybe not. The creative wheels in his head began to crank up for the first time in a whole day.

'Having fun?' Hannah asked from her prone position.

'Loads. You?'

'Mmm. Would it be a complete *faux pas* to ask why on earth mountains float your boat?'

The wheels ground to a halt. The wide-open feeling he'd been experiencing closed down as tight as a submarine preparing to submerge.

'Why not mountains?' he shot back, giving her the same line he'd given a thousand times over, in press interviews and private conversations alike.

Her stare was blank. 'That's all I'm going to get?'

After last night, was left unsaid.

Bradley shuffled his backside on the hard ground.

Hannah rolled her eyes, not even pretending she was happy to await an answer with unlimited feminine patience. 'Fine,' she said. 'Go into shutdown mode. Just remember you're the one who said what happens here stays here. I took that to mean my attempt at Karaoke last night and my mother's undie-flashing high-kick extravaganza, as well as any other private revelations we might encounter.'

He looked down at her prostrate form. She was right. He'd been privy to parts of her life she'd *clearly* have preferred to keep separate from her Melbourne life. He owed her something of the same. A glimpse, at the very least. Just so that at the end of this strange weekend there would be no debts owed.

He braced his hands against the cold hard ground and looked out at the breathtaking vista. 'Why mountains…?'

He felt her head roll his way.

'It goes something like this. When you climb a mountain solo, the challenge is so great, so seemingly impossible, the pay-off is all the sweeter when you reach the peak. You've conquered the unconquerable. Alone. The glory is yours alone.'

They sat in silence a few moments as his words disappeared in the thin air. Then Hannah said, 'But you also have no one to cheer you on when you succeed. No one to look out for you if you fall.'

He slid a quick glance her way.

She was looking at him, brows furrowed. Interested, but concerned. Those pale green eyes were seeing far too much. Wanting too much from him.

How much would it take to negate Virginia's undie-flashing high-kicks? More than something he'd just as readily reveal to a journo, surely?

He cleared his throat and began slowly, the words unfamiliar and uncomfortable on his tongue. 'I've grown used to not having anyone cheer me on. Or care if I fall. In fact I prefer it that way.'

'I know you do. What I don't understand is why?'

He swallowed hard, his throat parched to the point of pain. He couldn't do this. Shouldn't have to. It was none of her damned business.

She dragged herself to sit and waited till he glanced her way. 'I miss having my dad tell me, "That's my girl," when I do something fantastic. I even miss my mother *tsking* when she had to bandage an unladylike scraped knee. I can live without them, but it's nice to know that if I ever need that kind of support I have friends who care about me, who'll come to my rescue. You do too, you know. You only have to let them.'

Bradley shook his head. 'It's my experience that you can never count on anyone but yourself.'

'What experience?' she pressed.

'Formative experience,' he allowed.

'So try again.'

'I can't.'

'Why not?'

The woman was like a dog with a bone!

He turned on her. 'You really want to know?'

'I really want to know.'

'Fine,' he said, the overly loud word echoing across the cavernous space. Then like shots from a rifle, he hit her with his father's departure before he was born. His mother's continued indifference. The day she'd decided looking after him was simply too hard. The plethora of addresses he'd temporarily inhabited. The way in which he'd seen people turn a helpless kid out of their home simply for the sake of ease.

Then suddenly the instances became more specific. Names, faces, places, dates. One draining disillusionment after another.

It was only after some time that he realised she'd curled a gloved hand through his elbow. Offering the kind of support she'd promised he'd have if he just asked.

'Do you see her much any more? Your mum?'

'I looked for her once,' he said, the words all but pouring from him now. 'When I was in my twenties. I'd made some money. I'd bought some real estate. I'd proved to myself that I was worth something. And the need to let her know it too built and festered inside of me until I had no choice but to track her down.'

Hannah gently leant her head against his bicep. Where others might have shuffled and fidgeted and changed the subject, she just absorbed. Like a sponge. He felt himself siphoning comfort from her, but rather than feeling guilty he sensed that she was utterly willing to give it. He felt no inclination to move away.

'I wrote her a letter. She wrote back. We agreed to meet. I turned up at the rendezvous. I saw her through the window on the street. It had been years, but I knew it was her in a second. She didn't look inside the restaurant. Never saw me sitting there. Never even made it through the front door. She was swallowed up by the sidewalk crowd and that was the last I ever saw of her.'

As he relived the moment inside his head he waited for it to burn, to hurt so deeply that he'd learned to close down his emotions so as never to feel so dependent on someone else's opinion of him ever again. Instead he felt a mild ache, a distant sorrow. Soothed by the cooling balm of Hannah's light touch.

They sat like that for some time. No sound bar the wind whistling through the low scrub at their feet. Watching a lone eagle soar across the bright blue sky in a beautiful dance.

'I know now it wasn't about me,' he said. 'It never had been. Whatever her issues were, no matter how good I was, how successful, how sensible, it would never have been enough.'

Then Hannah said, 'So, no singing into your mother's hairbrush?'

And he laughed. Loud. Hard. Releasing laughter. Whatever remaining tension there was inside him cracked across the valley like a thunderclap.

'No,' he said. 'Not that I can remember.'

Her hand slipped from his arm, and ridiculously—considering how well-dressed he was—he suddenly felt the cold.

She buried her face in her hands. 'God, I feel like such an idiot for whining about Virginia's maternal deficiencies. At least she tried. Not well, mind you, but there *was* effort. Why didn't you just tell me earlier to shut up and stop feeling so sorry for myself?'

Why? Because he'd never told anybody. Because he'd never wanted to reveal that weakness in his genes. Because he thought she had every right to be upset at her mother's behaviour.

She turned to smile at him. Then gave his shoulder a bump with hers as she said, 'Thank you.'

'For what?'

She shrugged. But didn't stop smiling.

That mouth. He couldn't for the life of him remember what had convinced him to yabber on when all he had to do was lose himself in that mouth.

The urge to kiss her then was a primal one. Swelling from deep inside. The urge to pull off her beanie and run his fingers through her hair. To slide his thumbs across those soft pink lips. To follow with his mouth. His tongue. To lie her down gently on the mossy ground and make love to her until night fell...

And they froze to death.

For a man whose best interests were his only compass, he felt as if he was no longer exactly sure which way was north.

As though she sensed he'd hit his limit, Hannah blithely changed the subject. 'I can't believe my little sister is getting married tomorrow.'

'Does it feel strange that she got there first?'

'Strange...? No. God, no. I've seen how it can turn out when it's done with no thought, no plan, no certainty. Case in point: my mother. I'm more cautious, I guess. I don't have Elyse's…blind faith. Besides, I'm a career woman, don't you know?'

He laughed softly. 'Good to know.'

She tipped her beanie.

She leant over and grabbed the toes of her boots. 'So, while we're on the subject, tell me how come some gorgeous, sparkly, doe-eyed young starlet didn't snap you up long ago?'

He shot her a glance, but she was still mighty intrigued with her boots.

'Who says I even *like* gorgeous, sparkly, doe-eyed… Okay. I'm gonna stop there, before I sound like an idiot.'

'Too late,' she grumbled.

But while her voice was light he heard the tremor beneath. Her question hadn't been blasé. She wanted to know. Because she was one of the people around him who cared.

He had to make sure she never made the mistake of caring too much.

'I like women,' he threw back. 'But I like being single more. I've always been perfectly transparent on that score. And I've yet to have any woman cling to my ankles as we parted ways. I like to think I've found my perfect balance.'

Hannah picked up a piece of shale and scraped at a tuft of grass. 'Did it ever occur to you that they leave thinking themselves lucky to have had you at all? Even if just for a moment? And that your "transparency" made it impossible for them to wish for more?'

He glanced at Hannah to find she was still super-interested in her shoes. He could have sworn her cheeks had grown pinker. And she was nibbling at her bottom lip.

Suddenly he could hear his blood pumping fast and furious in his ears.

'So you think I'm a catch?' He'd meant it as a joke, a tension-breaker. But his tone came out deadly serious. He wanted to know her answer. Needed to know. Because if this was already more to her than a weekend fling...

Hannah froze. So small beneath her many layers. She slowly lifted her head to squint at the horizon. 'To be a catch one first has to be caught.'

'Don't hide behind semantics,' he growled, temper rising, cursing her for not following the rules.

She turned on him, eyes gleaming. 'Fine. Then I can see why *some* people might think you're a catch. Rich, famous, okay-looking in the right light.'

'But not you?'

She rolled her eyes at the gods—asking for help, or perhaps for a lightning bolt to strike him where he sat. 'You forget,' she said, 'we've worked together too long. I know you far too well, Bradley—on your good days and your bad—to indulge in such daft fancy.'

His eyes bored into hers. Looking for a twinkle of humour. Or, at the other end of the spectrum, a straight out lie. But for once he could decipher nothing within the pretty green flecks.

He was left feeling finessed. Deflected. It was the strangest, most off-kilter sensation, not being the one holding all the cards. He didn't like it.

'Lucky for you you're too smart for me.'

'Lucky for you too.'

To all intents and purposes things were back on track. Unease settled on his shoulders all the same. He pulled himself to stand and stretched out his back, which was stiff with a tension that had nothing to do with the hike or the cold.

He held out a hand and helped her to stand. She attempted to brush herself down but, considering she was so padded he could probably roll her back down the hill, she couldn't reach half of her back.

He spun her around and briskly brushed the grass from her well-cushioned backside. She stood there and let him. Despite everything he felt himself getting aroused. Hell, three layers of clothes and he could *still* have brushed that backside all day and all night.

He pulled his hand back into the protection of his jacket sleeve and headed back down the trail, towards the lake, towards the Gatehouse, towards their suite.

Friction followed in his wake, and its name was Hannah.

All he knew was the second they got behind closed doors all that tension would translate into passion, and they'd not be able to get their hands on one another soon enough.

He curled his gloved fingers into his palm. He craved her enough to allow her to see into his well-protected past. He craved her so much he'd take her despite his niggling concern about her motivation.

She'd become an addiction. One he'd convinced himself he could go cold turkey on in three days' time. When they'd be back to working side by side, ten hours a day, six days a week. When late at night, after everyone had gone, he'd sit at his desk, looking over the Melbourne skyline, with the lingering scent of her playing havoc with his senses.

'Speaking of work…' he said.

'I wasn't aware we had been,' she said, closer behind than he'd thought she'd be. Apparently she was in as much of a hurry as he to get back to their suite.

He slowed till they walked side by side. 'I was thinking earlier about taking Spencer on the Argentina trip.'

'Oh. Okay. Great. He'll be so excited—'

'Instead of you.'

A spark of hurt flashed across her eyes. His gut clenched unexpectedly. It only made him more determined. He held his ground. This was important. Important he do this now. Before things got any more complicated than they already were.

'Why?'

Because you care too much, and I clearly count on you too

much, and we're both setting ourselves up for disappointment, he thought.

He said, 'He did everything I asked of him yesterday, and well. I thought I ought to see how he goes with more responsibility.'

'Right. That's fair. But *I* set up that meeting. You wouldn't even be going if I hadn't wooed the Argentinians in the first place. I had to stay by the phone till after midnight every night for two weeks so as to be able to take their calls. I went above and beyond for—' Voice getting breathless, she pulled up short and shook her head. 'Why am I bothering? Do what you want. You always do. You're the boss.'

'Glad you remembered that.'

The look she shot him could have cut glass.

'Because, as your boss, I have a job for *you* to do.'

'Tell someone who's not on holiday,' she threw over her shoulder, and she took off down the path in front of him, her ponytail swinging accusingly at him.

He lifted his voice so as to be heard through the thin air. 'When we get back I want you to concentrate on putting together a full proposal for the Tasmania project. Locations. Treatment. Budget. Marketing. Everything.'

Her feet kicked up dust as she screeched to a halt. A full five seconds later she turned and stared up at him. 'Are you serious?'

'Have you ever known me to kid about work?'

'You? Never. Sonja and I behind your back? Every damn day.' Expression deadly serious, she took three steps up the hill and jabbed a finger into his chest. 'Now, let me get this straight. If I'm creating the project specs from scratch...'

'You'll be producing it.'

She shoved her hands into the pockets of her parka and breathed in, obviously thinking very deeply. The longer the moment passed, the more Bradley began to fidget. He'd expected her to leap into his arms with joy. He hadn't expected her to consider it. Or, worse, ponder why.

She spun on the spot. Jabbed him in the chest again. Then took a step back. Her eyes widened as she seemed to lose purchase on the loose ground. And suddenly she was halfway to head over heels.

Bradley reached out and grabbed her by the parka, his fingers clenching tight around the handful of slippery fabric while she wavered at a terrifying angle.

She glanced behind her and let out a cry. 'Bradley!'

'I know.' He could see the ground dropping away. He didn't even want to know the kind of angle she saw.

His fingers ached. Sweat broke out over his forehead. He dug his heels into the ground and, gritting his teeth, all but broke through the outer lining of her jacket in order to haul her back to safety.

She fell into his arms, breathing like a racehorse and shaking like a leaf.

He growled, 'You scared me half to death.'

'How do you think *I* feel?'

He couldn't help himself. He laughed. The sound ricocheted off the surrounding cliffs. It was either that or hold her so tight she'd begin to get ideas.

'So glad you can take my near death so lightly,' she said. 'I'm sure there are *some* who would miss me if I never made it back to Melbourne.'

He breathed deep through his nose and scraped her away from his front to look down into her face. 'Sonja would miss you once her heat got turned off.'

'True.'

'And Spencer. He'd be devastated.'

'He would. But that's all? That's some epitaph. Hannah Gillespie, twenty-five and single, falls to dramatic death from mountain. Terribly missed by semi-estranged family, chilly roommate, and dorky work-experience kid.'

Laughing, Bradley reached out and stroked the back of a finger across her cheek, sweeping her hair away from her eyes. When a strand remained she blew it out of the way with a shot of air from the side of her mouth.

Her eyes remained locked to his. All but begging for him to put her out of her misery and admit *he'd* miss her.

If she only knew how much. More than was in any way sensible. And it wasn't just about her work ethic. It was so very much about the lightness she lent to the rigours of his days.

'Remind me to chastise you for utter stupidity later. But for now...'

He crushed his mouth to hers and kissed her, and kissed her, and kissed her, until the ferocious force of their chemistry took over and nothing else mattered but how soon they could get back to the hotel.

Hannah got back to the room first, as Bradley had been forced to stay behind and read a half-dozen messages at Reception. She could have waited, but the excuse to take a moment apart was welcome.

She tore off her gloves, beanie, scarf, parka and shoes, and stretched out suddenly far lighter limbs as she padded into the room in jeans and long-sleeved T.

But no stretching could negate the confusion that was rocketing through her. She felt more as if she'd spent the past few hours on a rollercoaster rather than a mountain hike. Her roiling stomach could certainly attest to that.

Bradley sharing things from his past she'd never hoped he might impart. While still keeping his emotional distance any time she tried to close the gap.

Bradley offering her a chance at the Tasmania show. While unceremoniously ditching her from the Argentina pitch.

Bradley looking at her as if he wanted to devour her on the spot. While reminding her in no uncertain terms that the devouring wouldn't go on past that weekend.

Bradley, beautiful and bombastic and in his element.

No wonder the documentary-maker who'd discovered him halfway up K2, camera in hand, strong, beautiful face peering out from beneath a month's worth of dark facial hair, looking like the first real man on earth, had appeared unable to control her salivation when asked in the press about that fateful day. The day that introduced the mountaineer to television and Bradley Knight to an unprepared world.

Up, down. Up, down. Her emotions felt so twisted her heart had yet to stop beating as if she'd run a marathon.

Feeling prickly, and fractious, and uncooperatively turned on, Hannah trudged towards her room, stripping off more layers as she went. She passed near the spa. It twinkled darkly at her. As did her half-drunk glass of wine. And the discarded condom packet she'd torn open with her teeth.

And her father's watch bobbing in the water.

'No, no, *no*!' She ran around the edge of the pool and dropped to her knees, gathering it in her hands.

She'd been wearing it as she'd waited for Bradley to return. Had been wearing it still when she'd slipped into the pool. And now water drops sat suspended beneath the large face on which the hands hadn't moved since a little after three that morning.

'What's wrong?' Bradley's voice boomed from the doorway. Her cry must have been loud enough for him to hear it from the hall.

She shook her head. 'Nothing.'

He was at her back before she could scramble to her feet and walk away. To curl up in a ball and cry. In private.

'Hannah, I'm sorry, but I need to know that you're okay.'

She held up her watch. 'It's ruined.'

He glanced from her face to the watch, to the spa and back again. Then his whole body seemed to relax. 'Thank God. I thought you were hurt.'

Hannah recoiled as though slapped. Her voice rose as she

said, 'Did you not hear me say that my watch is ruined? It's dead.'

'Let me have a look.' He took the watch from her hands and checked it out under the light. 'Mmm... I'm not entirely sure it was built for underwater adventure. If you really need a watch there's a gift shop downstairs.'

She grabbed her watch back and cradled it in her palm. 'I don't want another watch. This was my dad's. It's the only thing of his I took with me when I left.'

Her heart squeezed. The turbulent tension of the afternoon was making it hard for her to see straight.

But it didn't matter. Bradley just stood there and said nothing. Doing his deer-caught-in-the-headlights impression. He might have been there for her on the side of the mountain, but the man clearly had no idea how to function in the face of real emotion.

It usually amused her when he froze up, as emotion was the only thing she'd ever seen him not do brilliantly. Right then it pissed her off royally. And instead of being able to revel in feeling pissed off she'd now found out *why* he was the way he was. His bloody mother had screwed him up for every other woman who came into his life.

Hannah had known he was stubborn. Known he was closed off. But the damage done had clearly affected every part of his life. If he couldn't trust his own mother, who could he trust? He was never going to commit. Not to anyone. Not to her.

In the next half-second everything came to a head. The build-up to her trip, her mother being her mother, having an affair with her boss, the fact that no matter what she did from that point her life in Melbourne would never be the same and, yeah, even the fact that her little sister was getting married before she'd even come close.

She felt angry. And hurt. And exposed. Like a great big throbbing nerve.

'Are you really going to just stand there and say nothing?' she asked. 'Nothing to try and make me feel like my heart *hasn't* just been torn from my chest? Can't you even pretend that you care about anything but yourself? Just for a second? You're killing me here!'

She didn't even realise she was pummelling his chest in a release of the most rabid frustration until he grabbed her by the wrists. Shaking still, she glared up at him, eyes burning so hot she might have been looking directly into the sun.

Slowly he lifted her hands and placed them on his shoulders. He didn't let go until they clamped down hard.

He placed his hands either side of her face, looked down into her eyes, stilling her, quieting her, making sure all she could think of was those eyes. That moment. That man.

His lips brushed hers with less pressure than a whisper. Again, and again, and again. Her bones turned to liquid. Her blood to molasses. She hadn't the energy to do anything but cling to him as he administered the most endearing kiss of her entire life.

Her earlier confusion and pain and frustration subsided as pleasure in its purest form took their place.

When he slid an arm beneath her knees and carried her into her bedroom she leant her head against his chest, taking solace from the heavy, steady beat of his heart.

He laid her gently on the bed. Carefully peeled her clothes from her warm body. And gazed at her for the longest time. She felt as if she was falling. From a great height. Even the touch of his eyes could send her spiralling over a precipice. Only he'd never be there to catch her emotionally. And it wasn't his fault. He simply wasn't equipped to know how.

He knelt over her—big, beautiful, a danger to her heart. He made love to her gently, slowly, with unbridled heat in his beautiful silver eyes. She didn't once care that he hadn't said a word. Hadn't eased her mind. Hadn't made any promises he couldn't keep.

How could she quibble when her body pulsed with a slow burn that steadily built until she felt as if she was made of pure fire?

Hannah woke up hours later, naked in bed, the room pitch-black. No moonlight gave her a sense of time or place. Only the warm thrum of her body reminded her who and where she was.

She carefully slid her foot sideways until it kicked a man's hairy calf. Bradley hadn't gone back to his own room. He'd stayed.

The kick must have unsettled him, for he rolled over, draping an arm across her waist, tucking his knees into the crook of hers.

She tucked her sheets to her chin and stared at the dark ceiling, her heart pounding, wondering how she was going to get through the next two days in one piece.

CHAPTER NINE

THE afternoon of the wedding Hannah stood staring at her reflection in the bathroom mirror.

After hours at the hands of myriad professionals, her hair hung in long lush waves, a portion kept from her face with the use of a delicate black and silver butterfly clip, and great big dark, smoky eyes looked back at her. Cheekbones most women would kill for. Soft, moist, bee-stung lips.

She looked…changed. But it had little to do with the makeover.

There was a relaxation of the constant furrow in her brow. An ease of movement that came with the most languid muscles in the world. All the make-up in the world couldn't do as much for a girl's complexion as a weekend spent in Bradley Knight's arms.

All of which was going to come to a screaming halt after the next day. After wishing this weekend would fly, she now found herself wishing it would stop speeding by so very fast.

She was swiping on one last layer of gloss on her lips when a light knock sounded at her bedroom door.

Bradley. Her heart sang. For a moment she had the strangest thought: *He's not meant to see me before the wedding!* A half-second later, when she remembered rightly that they were just bystanders in today's proceedings, she felt a right fool.

'Come in,' she called, shoving the lipgloss wand back into its tube.

Bradley didn't wait to be asked twice. He swept the door open and she caught a waft of his familiar scent on the rush of air. She breathed it as if it was an elixir.

Feigning fixing her hair, she shot him the quickest glance.

Black dinner suit cut to make the most of his broad angles. Hair slicked back. Freshly shaven.

He looked so unfairly beautiful she had to remind herself to breathe.

You've seen him in a dinner suit before, you goose! Many many times! In tuxes just as many. Heck, you've even tied his bow tie before shoving him into cars and off to attend glamorous awards nights.

Only those times it had been business. This time he was all dolled up to be her date. He'd *shaved* to be her date.

She widened her eyes at her reflection and silently told herself to cool it. He'd probably shaved because the mountain air was making him itch.

'There,' she said. 'Enough preening. That's about as good as it's going to get.'

She turned to face him, fully expecting to find him leaning indolently against the doorjamb, nonchalantly flicking a piece of lint from his jacket.

Instead he stood stock still, his broad body filling the doorway, shoulders stiff, jaw clenched, nostrils flared, hands in trouser pockets. He looked as if he wouldn't have had a clue if his entire suit was covered in lint.

His resolute gaze was locked onto her dress. The long full skirt swished at her toes, but it was the top half that him enthralled. From a twisting halterneck, heavy black fabric cut away at the sides, kissing the edge of her breasts and sweeping low at the back, to come together just above her buttocks, leaving her back completely bare.

She saw the moment it occurred to him that it left no room whatsoever for underwear bar the tiniest hipster G-string. His nostrils flared again, and he dragged his eyes shut. She even thought she heard a groan.

She summoned her inner imp to break the tension turning her insides to knots. She held out her skirt and let it fall in soft folds against her thighs. 'So, what do you think?'

Bradley opened his eyes. They followed the movement, and a muscle clenched in his jaw. 'You don't want to know what I'm thinking.'

'Try me.'

When his eyes finally locked onto her eyes she literally swayed towards him, so hot, so brutal, so intense was his expression.

Then his eyes glinted, and his beautiful mouth curved into a corrupting smile. He took a step her way.

She shuffled back—only to bang into the bench. Her fingers gripped the cold marble so hard they hurt.

And Bradley just kept on coming.

'I'm thinking about poor Roger,' he said.

'What?' Hannah shook her head, but she'd heard him right. 'You're thinking about *Roger*?'

'Poor kid's going to split a seam when he gets a load of you.'

'Oh.'

His covetous eyes caressed her throat, as if he was imagining burying his face right there.

The memory of just how it felt when he trailed deep hot kisses across her neck overcame her. Her head dropped back and she let out a long sigh.

At the sound his gaze locked on her mouth. If possible his eyes turned darker. Hotter. Harder. Completely absorbed. She snapped her mouth shut. All that carefully applied gloss…

All the while he continued edging closer, until he all but

filled the bathroom. His beautiful face gazed hungrily down at her from a half-dozen angled mirrors. There was no escape.

He came as close as he possibly could without actually touching her. She had to tilt her head to look at him. To be bewitched by the multiple shades of hot silver glinting in his eyes.

He rested his hand on the cold marble bench, his fingers mere millimetres from hers. She wasn't sure if it was the taste of her toothpaste or the scent of his that tickled her tongue. Either way, she licked her lips. And this time Bradley didn't even try to hide his groan.

'He has a crush on you, you know,' he said, his voice so raw, so deep, it rumbled through her body, leaving trails of goosebumps in its wake.

She blinked. 'Who?'

'Roger.'

She frowned. Again with Roger! She'd opened her mouth to tell him to forget about Roger, for Pete's sake, when finally she got it.

Bradley was using the guy as some kind of prophylactic in order to get her out of this small room without having her expensive, one-of-a-kind dress torn from her body an hour before her sister's wedding.

It was a heady feeling, knowing she could make a man feel that close to losing his grip. Bring him to the absolute cliff-face of sexual need. One touch and she had no doubt she could send him over the edge. The fact that she was doing all those things to *this* man...

Her body felt so quivery and hot her elbows threatened to give way. The sexual tension swirling about the room was intoxicating. It felt as if there was no more oxygen. As if the only way for her to breathe again was to fulfil the need clawing at her insides.

But, dammit, he was right about the dress! There was no

getting out of it, or around it, or beneath it, without ruining its soft folds.

She bit her lip. *Damn.* She'd have to redo her lip gloss. Then again, there was plenty more where that came from.

Without another thought she lifted up onto her toes and pressed her lips to his.

For a moment he resisted. He stared into her eyes and held firm. All that effort he'd put into keeping his hands off was binding him as tight as a corkscrew.

Fortunately she was a glass of champagne ahead of him, and not feeling nearly so well-behaved. She closed her eyes, tilted her head, and kissed him again. Slowly. Softly. Teasing him with the lightest flick of her tongue where his lips pressed together.

When her tongue met his she flinched, but only for the briefest of seconds. For finally he was kissing her back. His lips sliding against hers. His tongue tasting hers. Curling about it, toying with her, showing just how much control he had left in reserve.

After what felt like eons later he pulled away. Without his kiss holding her upright any more she leant her forehead against his chest.

'Apple-flavoured?' he asked, licking his lips.

She smiled at his tie. 'Tasmania is the Apple Isle.'

He laughed, and her stomach did a neat little backflip.

Then he stepped back. And frowned. 'Something doesn't look right.'

She spun to check her dress wasn't tucked into the back of her G-string. 'What?'

'I'm not sure. But I think something's missing.'

He pulled a bag from the gift shop from behind his back.

Her heart skipped and tripped and turned over on itself.

'Cradle Mountain playing cards?' she said, with a noncha-lance she was far from feeling. 'Souvenir soap? A really tiny towelling bathrobe? Though why I'd need any of those things at a wedding—'

'Shut up and open the damn thing.' He dangled the pretty green bag from a hooked finger.

Brow furrowed, she pulled out a large hinged box. Clueless as to what it might be, she opened it—and then forgot how to breathe. A hand fluttered to her heart.

'Bradley?' she said, glancing up at him.

He took the box from her hands. 'Here—allow me.'

And then with gentle hands he slid her father's watch over her wrist and clasped it. Only now it worked. And was a perfect fit rather than slipping up her arm every time she moved.

'I had Housekeeping suspend it over their industrial dryer in the hope that drying it out might do the trick. It did. Then I asked if they had a jeweller nearby, and they said there was one staying at the hotel as part of the high school reunion party. He took out a couple of links.'

The massive watch sat heavy and familiar on her arm, but her eyes were all for Bradley.

He laughed softly, then took her hand in his. 'Come on. We'd best be off. Time's marching on.'

She followed him out of the room. Let him hand her the beaded purse from the kitchenette bench and help her on with her flat silver sandals.

Time was marching on all too fast. She could practically hear the seconds booming inside her. Time till the weekend was over. Time till they flew back home in his jet. Till they went their separate ways at the airport. Till she reported for duty first thing Tuesday morning.

And went on as though nothing had happened.

As though they'd never made love.

Never been exposed to so much about one another's most private lives.

A strange kind of pain made itself at home beneath her ribs.

She rubbed at the spot with one hand, while smiling blithely at Bradley as he swept her out through the suite door.

Bradley stood next to Hannah, waiting for the lift to take them downstairs. He felt strangely shaken. And stirred.

Seeing Hannah back there, looking amazing in that knock-out dress, he'd felt such a riddle of emotions he hadn't been able to pin down a one. Till now. Now they joyfully lined up one after the other, mocking him.

He spared her a glance. Her face was tilted as she watched the numbers count down. The only giveaway that she was as tense as he was, was the deep rise and fall of her chest.

He ran a hand across his chin, looking for the familiar painful sharp rasp of day-old hair against his palm to knock him to his senses, and was surprised to find it so smooth.

He let his hand drop and glowered at his wavering reflection. *Why not get the girl a corsage, if you're going to act like a sixteen-year-old punk going to the prom?*

He needed to get some perspective back. And fast.

This was a fling. Nothing more. A bit of holiday fun.

For her it was holiday fun. She was the one on holiday. He was *meant* to be scouting the place for gorgeous, treacherous locations for a future gig. The only gorgeous, treacherous thing he'd had in his sights was five feet six and nibbling at her ridiculously sexy bottom lip.

The lift doors opened to reveal a handful of people already inside. He ushered Hannah inside, careful not to touch her. Hell, if he was really afraid that a touch would only lead to more then he was in more trouble than he'd thought.

She glanced at him, caught his eye and smiled. Her lovely green eyes grew dark and dreamy, her smile all too knowing, and every inch of exposed skin flushed pale pink.

Desire rocketed through him so hard and so fast he reached out to grip the hip-high rail for support.

He should have left the second he'd realised she had a

crush on him. Or at the very least the moment he'd sensed how unusually hard it was going to be to walk away. Enough was enough.

He'd put on a show at the wedding, so as not to embarrass her in front of her family. Then he'd feign urgent work and head off. Cut the weekend short. Organise his jet to pick her up the next night while he scored whatever seat he could get on the next commercial plane off the island.

And then Tuesday morning she'd be back at his side. On her favourite chair in his office, cowboy-boot-clad feet on the corner of his desk, eating store-bought Caesar salad with a plastic fork. And all he'd want to do was wipe his desk clean with one sweep of an arm and throw her down on the table and make love to her until the building shook.

What a wretched ruddy mess.

The lift stopped at Elyse's floor. Hannah was off to do her maid of honour duties. She turned to say something, glanced at her watch, then laughed softly. With a quick wave she lifted her skirt and walked from the lift.

Watching her walk away, he felt a strange tug somewhere in the vicinity of his chest. He rubbed the spot, figuring his recent feats of athleticism in the bedroom had pulled something.

Nevertheless, as the lift doors closed, inside Bradley's head he ran a long list of mountains he'd yet to climb, beginning with the tallest, hardest, steepest, and furthest away.

Hannah stared at a crack in the concrete balustrade on the balcony outside the bathroom in which Elyse was 'taking a moment'—which in Gillespie female speak was elegant for 'taking a whizz'.

She sniffed in a lungful of cold mountain air, checked her watch. The watch that had used to be her father's watch. Only now when she looked at it she saw the watch Bradley had rescued.

She saw that it was only five minutes till the wedding was

due to start. She'd reached to knock on the bathroom door when the door opened.

'Your man is a beauty.' Elyse slurred the words ever so slightly as she swanned out, continuing the one-sided conversation she'd been having when she first went in. She screwed up her face and held out her hands as if she was pinching an imaginary pair of cheeks. 'He's so big, and manly, and rugged. Rock-god-sexy, you know?'

Oh, Hannah knew. All too well. She had barely gone a minute that weekend not thinking exactly those thoughts. And more. In intimate remembered detail. But only four and a half minutes before Elyse was due to marry sweet Tim wasn't the time to agree.

When the bride-to-be spun around a turn and a half and began heading back into the bathroom, Hannah took her by the elbow and steered her right.

'Lyssy, hon, how much have you had to drink?'

'Just a glass of champagne. I was feeling so anxious I thought I might throw up. And Mum'd kill me if I got anything on this dress.'

Right. Okay. *This* she could handle. In fact it was the most blissfully perfect time for a mini-crisis. She so needed something to take her mind off Bradley. And the watch. And the way he'd looked at her in the lift. And the inconveniently persistent glow that had refused to abate since she woke up that morning.

Time to get her sister married.

Her brave little sister.

Hannah wanted the real thing one day too. She really did. But she couldn't escape the niggling doubts. What if you stopped loving him? What if he didn't love you enough? What if you loved him more than life itself and he died?

Elyse flumped down onto a concrete bench. Hannah winced. If she didn't get moss stains on the masses of ivory silk it would be a miracle.

'Do you think it's possible to love one man your whole life?' Elyse asked. 'To be happy sleeping with one man for the rest of your days? Or the rest of his? Or…you know what I mean.'

Hannah knew exactly what she meant. *Look at Mum—do you think we have her genes?* She sat down carefully next to her sister and took her by the hand.

'I'm not sure I'm the one to ask. I've never been in love before.'

Elyse's eyes opened wide. 'Never?'

Hannah shook her head.

'Not even with Mr Heaven in Blue Jeans out there? Jeez, you have high standards.'

Did she? Was that the problem? She knew she'd moved on from men because they didn't give her that all-important spark, or make her laugh, or have anything brilliant to say, or their fingernails were a weird shape, or their forearms were too short. She'd always told herself she was simply waiting to find everything she wanted in one man. The truth was she'd already found it. In Bradley. Even thinking his name took the warm glow inside her to an all-time high, and Hannah's cheeks heated so fast she felt slightly dizzy.

Then Elyse's bottom lip began to tremble, and she gratefully switched her focus back to the bride. 'Lyssy? Are you okay?'

'I wish Dad was here.' Two great fat tears fell down her cheeks.

Hannah's lungs clenched so hard it physically hurt. She swallowed down the lump that had formed instantly in her throat. Blinked away her own tears. It had taken two long hours to do her make-up and she was not going through that again.

She turned to reach for her bag in search of tissues, but Elyse's loud echoing sniff stopped her. Elyse didn't need tissues. She needed her big sister.

She wiped her sister's tears away with the pad of her finger. 'I miss him too. Every day. But you know what? He would be *so* proud of us today. Looking all glossy and glam. Me the high-flying Melbournian. You marrying the man you adore. His girls have done good.'

'We have, haven't we? One thing I remember is him telling me he wanted nothing more than for us to be happy. And I'm happy. Really happy. You're happy, right?'

Hannah blinked. Was she happy? Much of the time. Could she be happier? You bet.

'Bradley would make you happy,' Elyse said, mirroring her thoughts so closely Hannah wondered if she'd said so out loud. 'At least tell me he's good in bed.'

Good? As words went, it was not even the correct language with which to describe what being with Bradley was like. French could maybe do it. Or Italian. Definitely Italian.

'Those long fingers…' Elyse shivered.

'Elyse!'

But Elyse was looking at her with such hope she couldn't deny her. Not on her wedding day.

'Fine. He's… It's better than I ever imagined it could be.'

'Then marry him!'

Hannah shook her head. Then shrugged. How could she explain to a woman about to marry the love of her life the sad little 'what happens in Tasmania' deal she'd made in order to get whatever scraps she could from the guy? 'I don't matter right now. Your life is yours. Not mine. Not Mum's. So, Miss Bride, are you ready to go become Mrs Tim Teakle?'

'I am,' Elyse answered without hesitation. 'I love him so much it hurts, with the most beautiful kind of ache right in the centre of my heart. It makes me want to laugh and twirl and sing. He makes me glow all over.'

'Then what else is there to do but go out there and marry the guy?'

Elyse threw her arms around her and they hugged. Tight. For an age.

Hannah closed her eyes and tried to block out the realisation that Bradley was the only man she'd ever known who made her want to laugh and twirl and sing. And she was glowing so hard right then she could barely see straight.

Something tumbled inside her, as though she'd accidentally stumbled upon the final part of a combination lock.

Oh, hell no. She *loved* him, didn't she?

She loved how he made her think. How he made her melt. Even how he made her halfway to crazy. He stretched her to her very limits and beyond.

She squeezed her eyes shut tighter as a bittersweet pain sliced through the glow.

The previous night, just before they'd made love, she'd run her hand down his stubbled cheek, looked him in the eye, and said out loud the words she was trying to use to convince herself. 'You're *so* the wrong guy for me.'

Bradley's eyes had darkened. Then he'd all but lit up as he'd smiled and said, 'Don't you ever forget it.'

She loved him. But what did that matter when he was too damaged and too stubborn to love her back? What was she going to do?

What *could* she do but go out there and be the most supportive maid of honour ever? Do everything in her power to avoid Bradley so that he'd never, *ever* have a single clue how she felt. Excellent plan.

Then Hannah saw the time. 'We're late!'

Elyse pulled away and straightened herself up. Then with a grin she settled back on the bench and said, 'I love him to pieces, but it can't hurt to keep him wondering just a little, right?'

Hannah sniffed out a laugh. Elyse clearly missed their dad as much as she did, but by God she was her mother's daughter.

* * *

Bradley lounged in one corner of a pink velvet chaise against a wall of the Gatehouse ballroom.

Above him a pink chandelier jiggled gently in time with the music. Beside him pink peonies floated in a crystal bowl filled with water. He was drinking coffee from pink floral Royal Doulton china. Elyse and Tim's wedding was the place pink had come to die.

The speeches were over. The cake was cut. The guests were a few champagnes down. 'Time Warp' blared from the speakers. The post-wedding party had well and truly begun.

But he didn't much care what the other guests were up to. There was only one he was searching for. One who seemed to have slipped through his grasp a good dozen times that day, with the excuse of having something else maid of honourly to do.

'Time Warp' finished, and the sexy drum beat of 'I Need You Tonight' belted out. The older dancers fled for water and chairs, while the young ones cheered and danced on. Young ones including the bride and, with her, a sleek brunette in a backless black dress.

Elyse might well have inherited her mother's dance floor skills, but Bradley would never know. His eyes remained locked on Hannah.

Or, more specifically, on the sway of her hips that had nothing to do with skill or lessons and everything to do with her innate sensuality. On the creamy flash of leg when the split of her skirt swished just the right way. The way she tossed her long hair with the same complete and utter abandon she showed in bed.

Every sensuous move reminded him of how it felt having her wrapped around him, how her warm skin gave beneath his touch, how right it sounded when she breathed his name as she fell apart in his arms.

She raised her arms in the air. Eyes closed. Completely

unaware of the pack of men dancing as near as they could get to her without alerting their dates.

A swan in a duck pond. She didn't fit in there any more—if she ever had. She had outgrown the people and the place. She'd never stay.

He'd followed her and hijacked her holiday so as to make sure she'd return to Melbourne. He was now sure she would. He'd stayed in order to make sure she had a good time—in order to carry out his thanks for all her hard work. He was more than certain she had. If they were the only reasons he was there, he might as well just leave a message with someone that he'd left, then turn and walk away.

He put his coffee on the table and leant forward, bracing his hands on his knees. Then he sat back in his seat. *Dammit*.

'It's bad form to leave before the bride and groom.'

Bradley turned to find Hannah's mother sinking down onto the other end of the chaise, a vision in apple-green. If she'd intended to stand out against the sea of pink, she'd succeeded.

'You've outdone yourselves today, Virginia. I know a class production when I see one.' He held out a hand to give hers a congratulatory shake. She slid a glass of beer into it instead. She lifted her own in salute, and downed half in one go.

Bradley took a more conservative sip. By the look in the woman's sharp eyes he had a feeling he was going to need to be sober for what was about to come.

'I know your type,' she said.

And we're off.

'What type is that?'

'You're a player. Not a stayer. I know because, bar one, I've been drawn to men just like you my entire life.'

'This concerns you how?'

She stared at him, her eyes a different colour from her daughter's but with the same intensity.

Bradley placed his beer on the table and looked out into the crowd. 'Bad form or not, would you prefer me to leave?'

Virginia laughed. 'Please. Do I look like a bouncer?'

Bradley spared her a glance. She looked like trouble, not the mother of the bride. But she was also Hannah's mother. As such, he had no intention of getting into a sparring match.

'Nevertheless...' he said, rising to leave.

She placed a taloned hand on his knee and pressed down hard. 'I see the way you look at my daughter.'

He didn't dignify what was clearly meant as an accusation with a response. Though his eyes did slide straight to the dance floor. Hannah had disappeared yet again. He swore beneath his breath.

'Elyse is far more like me,' Virginia continued. 'She's a shrewd operator. She swam through sharks to find her sweet minnow. As for Hannah? There's not a cunning bone in that girl's body. She plays fair, tries hard, and assumes that will lead her to green pastures. In life, work and love. So much her father's daughter that one. Sees the good in everyone—even those who don't deserve it.'

Bradley's head suddenly felt tight, as if it was being pressured from a dozen different directions. He looked to Virginia, who was watching him like a hawk. He said, 'If you're about to ask my intentions with regard to Hannah, you're going to be disappointed. I am a private person, and as such my business is not open for discussion.'

'Bradley?'

Bradley looked up to find Hannah standing over them. Tousled, pink-cheeked, gorgeous. His blood warmed ten degrees just looking at her. The woman who'd been avoiding him all day.

Then he saw her brow was furrowed in concern, while her eyes flicked between him and her mother. She must have felt the tension fair across the room.

'Everything okay?' Hannah asked.

'Fabulous. Sit,' Virginia said, patting the space between

them on the chaise. 'Bradley was just telling me this is the best wedding he's ever been to. Weren't you, Bradley?'

Hannah looked at him, eyebrows dipping deeper. 'Did he also mention this is the *first* wedding he's ever been to?'

Virginia laughed as if it was the funniest thing she'd ever heard. 'He did not. In fact he's been quite tight-lipped about a good many things. Such as what the two of you think you're up to.'

'All righty,' Hannah said, her tone impatient. Then she grabbed Bradley by the hand and hauled him to his feet. 'Come on, boss. I feel like dancing.'

'Darling,' Virginia drawled, 'I just want to get to know your friends.'

'Leave it alone, Virginia. I mean it.' Then Hannah's hand wrapped tight around his and she put herself bodily between him and her mother. As if she was saying, *If you want to take a swing at him you'll have to go through me.*

What a woman. Five feet six and fifty kilos dripping wet, protecting *him*, six feet four inches of hard-won muscle on muscle.

No wonder she was so good at absorbing the million little dramas a day that came his way at work. Making his life seem easier just by being around. She'd been doing it her whole life. Only now, rather than seeing it as to his advantage, he wondered how many hits she'd have to take before she stopped feeling them. Stopped feeling anything. Before that beautiful bright Hannah light disappeared for ever.

He held her hand tight and curled it through his arm. Time someone absorbed the drama for *her* for a change.

'Lovely chatting to you, Virginia,' Bradley said.

She raised her glass in salute. 'Bradley. I hope you'll at least find the time to say a proper goodbye.'

The double meaning hit right where it was meant to. The jab of a mother protecting her kid the only way she seemed to know how.

'I'll do my best.'

Virginia nodded. Then turned and called out to another guest, insisting they join her for a 'drinkie'.

Hannah tugged Bradley's hand and yanked him towards the dance floor as though her life depended on it.

'What the heck was that all about?'

'What?'

Her expression was deadpan, then she just shook her head and let the music take her cares away.

And watching her sway, her tousled hair swinging, sexy muscles playing across her beautiful bare back, hips bopping in time with the music, he wondered what his drink had been spiked with if he'd even thought about cutting this weekend a second shorter than it could be.

He tugged her into his arms, slid a hand down her back, and breathed deep as she trembled at his touch.

One more day.

CHAPTER TEN

A SLOW song began.

Bradley saw Roger nearby, hitching his pants and fixing his bow tie, slicking back his ridiculously preppy blond hair, Hannah firmly in his sights.

He swung Hannah out to the end of his arm and growled, 'This one's mine,' in the kid's ear, before sweeping Hannah back into his arms.

With a sigh she didn't even try to hide, Hannah slid her hands up his chest, over his shoulders and around his neck. He fought the intense shudder her touch created, but there was no stopping it.

'I can't believe it's night already. The wedding's over. Elyse made it up the aisle. Tim didn't faint. Mum has yet to try to take the stage. Things couldn't have gone better. And then, I have to say, *this* is very nice,' she said, her voice husky as hell, her fingers playing gently with the hair at the back of his neck.

He wrapped her tighter. His erection pressed into her stomach. She made no mention of it, even though there was no way she could avoid the heat and hardness of him through the thin fabric of her dress. She just shimmied and swayed and smiled, and waved to familiar faces dancing past.

There was no way he was walking off the dance floor with that kind of action going on in his pants. But unfortunately having this woman sliding her body against his meant it wasn't going anywhere either.

Only when she shook her long hair from her shoulders and glanced up at him, a telling gleam in her eyes, did he realise she knew. And she was revelling in it. Then the minx only moved more softly, more sweetly against him.

He slid one hand into her hair and the other lower, down the gentle curve of her back and to the more daring curve below.

Take that.

Her pupils dilated till her eyes were dark as night. While sexual attraction sparked within them as bright and infinite as stars.

Then she waved to a guy on the other side of the room.

'Who was that?'

She sighed. 'Simon. High school crush.'

He pulled back just enough to see into her eyes. 'Shall I leave the two of you alone?'

'Too late. He's married with four kids.' She leant her head against his chest and hummed blissfully, almost standing on his foot every few steps.

'To think,' he said, pulling her hand into his shoulder, 'that could have been you.'

'Doubtful. He runs his dad's hardware store. He was never going anywhere. After Dad died I just never fit in here.' With a flick of her thumb towards the door she said, 'I was outta here the minute I had enough money saved.'

'Looking for adventure?'

Her fingers slid deeper into his hair and stayed there. Her voice was soft when she said, 'Looking for something.'

Like that, they swayed for a good long while. Lost in their own thoughts while caught up together in a familiar, inescapable swirl of sexual tension that only grew as they pressed closer, found ways to tuck more tightly into one another and caress each other till it ached.

Bradley couldn't take it any longer. 'Can we get the hell out of here?'

She raised her heavy head from his chest, her eyes dark and drowsy, as she said, 'I just have one last maid of honour job to do, then I'm off duty. You know what? It's one that you could help with.'

'Having seen inside your "just in case" suitcase, I'm understandably nervous about saying yes before I know what I'm getting myself into.'

She grinned. 'It involves masses of rose petals, bubble bath, champagne and condoms.'

'Then, hell, yeah.'

Moonlight shone through the unadorned bedroom window, leaving the room bathed in an eerie silver light.

Bradley wasn't sure how long he'd been awake, a pillow cradled behind his head as he watched Hannah sleep. Her skin was baby-soft, her cheeks pink from the heat of the still flickering fire he'd lit after the first time they'd made love. A slight frown puckered her brow, and her hair splayed out over the snow-white pillowcase.

And all he could think was that tomorrow things would be back to the way they'd been.

With one undeniable difference.

She wasn't like other women he'd been with. She wasn't cynical and nonchalant and insanely independent. She was sweet, sincere, loyal, and clearly not the type to indulge in a holiday fling.

He'd known that before he'd started this thing with her. He'd known it before he'd set foot on Tasmanian soil. Hell, he'd known it the minute Sonja had suggested the idea at that café in faraway Melbourne.

Yet he'd still let it happen.

He could blame the ridiculously decadent suite. He could blame the rugged beauty and unbelievably fresh air of Tasmania. Or he could blame Venus and Mars.

He could blame the lightness inside her, the ready laughter

and easy joy that contrasted so blatantly with the darkness of his own experiences. He could blame the fact that she gave him balance. Balance he'd never before had. Balance he secretly savoured.

But the truth was her mother had been right. He was a player, not a stayer. Worse, he was a rotten no-good bastard who didn't deserve to be defended the way this woman had leapt to his defence.

He had nobody to blame but himself.

She muttered something in her sleep, and then finished off with a husky laugh. He hated himself even as the sound of her laughter made him grow hard for her again.

He slid the back of a finger beneath a swathe of dark hair on her forehead, and then let his finger trail down her cheek, behind her ear, to that sensitive spot in the dent at her shoulder.

She stirred, stretching bent arms over her head, legs to the foot of the bed, collecting the sheet with them and revealing her naked torso. Her gently rounded breasts. Her soft, smooth nipples.

The ache in his gut was so convoluted, so heavy, so deep, he had no desire to spend any time discerning what it meant. Instead he leaned over and took one warm rose-pink peak into his mouth.

She groaned. Awake in an instant. Her hands clamping into his hair.

She tasted like caramel and sunshine. It was nothing less than cruel that a woman could taste so good. He closed his eyes as his tongue continued to circle her nipple until she was all but crying out, while holding his head to the spot as if she never wanted him to stop.

He rolled until he was on top of her, using the strength in his arms to stop himself crushing her, while his tongue delved into the shadow at the base of her other breast, then licked slowly and thoroughly upwards without touching her nipple.

As she writhed beneath him, pressing her warm flesh against him, he felt such an urge to plunge himself into her, again and again, until all rational thought was lost to the red mist of pleasure.

It took every ounce of strength he had to keep himself propped on his shaking arms. He'd done nothing to deserve giving in to his raging desires. He deserved to be punished.

He slid to her side. She groaned in protest, her back arching, a hand sliding down his arm, across his chest, scraping through the arrow of hair leading to his...

He closed his eyes. If this was punishment, send him to hell.

He grabbed her hand and restrained it over her head. Using a heavy leg, he pinned her writhing body to the bed.

Breathing heavily, eyes closed, she stopped moving, clearly doing her best to stay put, as though she knew it would be worth it to do as she was told. She was one clever girl.

The pale skin of her breast was shining from his ministrations, and slowly, achingly slowly, he lowered his head until he took her dry, peaked nipple into his mouth.

He worked his way down the sweetest spots of her body until he couldn't stand it any longer. There was no way he could last another minute without enjoying that mouth.

Look at me, he demanded inside his head. He wanted her to know who was kissing her. He needed her to know. To remember.

She opened slumberous eyes and looked right into the dark depths of his soul. Then, as if she knew just what he needed she pulled his head to hers and kissed him.

The sun was just starting to send its pink glow through the floor-to-ceiling windows when Hannah quietly threw on jeans, T-shirt, poncho and boots, scrunched her hair back in a ponytail and quickly washed her face before tiptoeing out of the suite.

She needed a walk. A walk and a think. And clearly she didn't do her best thinking when Bradley was lying sprawled out naked in her bed.

The *bing* of the lift was overly loud in the pre-dawn quiet. She glanced back at the door leading to their suite, but it stayed closed.

Once downstairs, she padded across the empty reception area and straight out through the front doors. The whip of cold slapped her across the face so sharply she almost stumbled. But that morning it was just what she needed.

Outside the sky was silvery grey, the trees stark and brown, the ground a winter wonderland. The air was still, the birds asleep, the only sound the soft fall of snow from overladen trees.

It was like a dream.

She stood there, trying her very best to compartmentalise the whole weekend that way—to believe it was all a lovely dream and to understand that when she woke up the next morning she would be well and truly back in the real world.

Real life suddenly felt so foreign. So far away. And more than a little scary. All she had to do to fix that was convince Bradley that they should stay. For ever. Eating Room Service, having someone else wash the sheets, making love. Easy!

No. She couldn't tell him. How could she? When he'd made it clear again and again that he was not the settling kind of man? His past might have sown the seeds for that behaviour, but he'd cultivated it heartily ever since.

She couldn't tell him and have it thrown back in her face. There was nothing worse than having love with nowhere to put it. When her dad had died it had hurt like nothing else. Had broken things inside her. She'd wandered like a lost kitten for months. Years, even. Until she'd found her feet, her place, her*self* in Melbourne.

No matter which way she looked, neither of them had the stamina or the history to support anything long-term.

She sighed, and her breath puffed white. She rubbed a finger beneath her cold nose, wrapped her poncho tighter around her, and headed back into the blissful warmth.

Reception was no longer empty. A woman in a tight skirt, patterned tights, high boots and a mulberry wrap and matching beret was standing at the desk. She turned at the sound of the front doors swinging.

'Hannah.'

'Mum.' The endearment popped out before she had time to even think 'Virginia', but her mother seemed not to notice, so she didn't edit herself. Instead she slowly headed over her way.

Virginia glanced at the colossal clock suspended above her. 'What are you doing up so early?'

'Just taking a walk. Needed some fresh air. You?'

'Heading home.'

'Oh. But didn't they tell you that your room's paid up for one more day?'

'They did. But I don't think Elyse needs to come downstairs the morning after her wedding night to find her mother at breakfast, do you?'

'No,' she blurted. 'I don't. That's really thoughtful of you.'

Virginia laughed. 'To make myself scarce? Isn't it?'

A man returned to Reception with some paperwork which he slid to Virginia. She thanked him with a smile that made the guy blush to the roots of his hair.

Filling out her paperwork, Virginia said, 'And where's your plus one?'

Figuring there was no point denying they'd been...whatever they were, she said, 'Asleep.'

Virginia laughed. 'If I were you I'd make it my mission in life to be there when he wakes up.'

Hannah swallowed hard. If the choice was hers alone she'd want nothing more for evermore. She felt an unexpected urge to confide in her mum. But history clamped her mouth shut on the subject.

Instead she assembled a grin and said, 'Never fear, I'm heading back that way now.'

'You always were a smart girl. And as it turns out one heck of a wedding-planner. The weekend was simply divine.'

'Wasn't it?' Hannah said with a smile.

'Sophisticated, fun, and a party that'll go down in local folklore. All thanks to you.'

Hannah blinked, trying to find a path inside her woolly, chilly, early-morning brain that could make sense of receiving such praise from her mother. In the end she simply said, 'Thanks.'

Virginia brushed it off with an elegant shrug. 'I've a half dozen names and numbers of young local brides-to-be and mothers-of already clamouring for your services if you have it in mind to have a sea change. To come home.'

Hannah managed a half-hearted laugh. Until she realised Virginia appeared to be serious. Expectant. Hopeful, even. That she might *stay*?

Stay. Home. Near Elyse. Near where she grew up. Where people cared for her. Where she could work for someone who didn't work her crazy hard, or make her fall madly in love with him.

The temptation was so strong in that moment it was almost overwhelming. But a moment was all it was. If she stayed she'd be running away. Again. But since the first time she'd run and not looked back she'd grown up and made a life for herself. Not a perfect life, but it was all hers.

'Thanks, Mum, but I'm happy where I am.'

Virginia's hopeful smile disappeared, and was replaced by a grin. 'Good for you.' Then, 'I so worried about you when you were a kid. Head in the clouds, nose in a book, trailing around after your dad like a puppy.' She placed the pen on the desk and turned. 'I wanted to see the world so badly when I was young.

To live in the city and work in the arts. To be somebody. Don't get me wrong—I loved your dad, and never regretted a single decision I made when it came to choosing him. But I didn't want you girls to be stuck in a small town without having found the rare reason to stay that I had. All I ever wanted for you was to find that something special that made you stand out from the crowd so you had chances I never took.'

She reached out, her hand stopping an inch from tucking Hannah's hair behind her ear, before turning to the desk, grabbing a pen and signing her name on the hotel bill with a flourish. 'I'm so proud that you made it happen for yourself. That you're happy.'

As she stood there in the big deserted foyer, her mother's niceties spinning in her head, Hannah's limbs felt numb—and it had nothing to do with the cold. It was as though that weekend her whole life had been tipped on its head.

Worried she'd never again know which way was up, or which way right, she knew she had to set things straight. Right then.

'Mum?'

'Yes, darling.'

'Can I ask you something...difficult?'

Virginia turned, a devilish grin in her eyes. 'Have you ever met a more difficult woman than me?'

Well. No.

'Okay. Here goes. When you married those...other guys, was it because you thought you loved them the way you'd loved Dad? Did you only find out later you were wrong?'

'No,' her mother answered without hesitation. 'Not even for a second.'

'Then why?'

Virginia took a breath, tapping a manicured finger against her bottom lip. Then she looked Hannah in the eye. Crow's feet fanned out from her beautiful eyes. Too much make-up covering what was still lovely skin.

'The truth is I miss what it feels like to be that loved. And if I can only get that in fits and spurts for the rest of my life, then that's what I'm willing to accept.'

That was what her beautiful, vibrant mother had to resort to? The scraps of love's leftovers? The very idea was reprehensible.

Hannah reached out and took her mother by the arm. 'You're worth more than that.'

Virginia looked at Hannah's hand.

'I mean it. No more settling. Find someone you love. Someone who loves you. And do whatever it takes not to let him go. Okay?'

Virginia smiled, but made no promises. Instead she leaned in and gave Hannah a kiss on the cheek. And fast on its heels came a hug. An honest to goodness hug.

'See you at the next wedding, kid. Even I half hope it will be yours.'

And then, with a wink, Virginia was gone, flouncing through the revolving doors in a swirl of energy and colour. And the sorrow of missing her first true love.

Hannah's mind fled the foyer. It was inside a hotel suite, where lay a man she loved to desperation.

She had always known she would never settle. Only for the first time she realised what that really meant. She wasn't going to settle for a man she *liked*. A man who ticked the boxes of what a husband *should* be. She wanted a lover, a partner, someone who made her laugh and made her think, a great and loyal friend she trusted with her life.

She wanted Bradley.

Hannah had everything she'd ever hoped and dreamed of right there at her fingertips. Right now. She couldn't let herself worry about the outcome. If she didn't at least try to have it all she'd never forgive herself.

Bradley was in the shower when Hannah got back to the suite. Humming something she couldn't put her finger on. Not a surprise. Her head was so full she could barely remember her own name.

She paced up and down his bedroom, prepping. Trying to figure the best way to tell him how she felt.

Casual? *Dinner? Saturday? My place? I promise not to cook.*

Blasé? *Let's shock the pants off everyone in the office and turn up tomorrow engaged.*

Sexy? *I want your hands inside my pants now, and a year from now. And I'm not taking no for an answer, big boy.*

Full frontal? *You're the one that I want!*

Honest?

Honest… She loved him. It was that simple. And that complicated. And that was what she needed him to know.

The bathroom door opened. She hadn't even heard the shower stop. Bradley stepped out, a large white towel slung low around his hips, feet bare. Water dripping from his dark hair. Wet muscles gleaming bronze in the low morning light.

Her mouth turned as dry as sand.

He started when he saw her standing in his room. Then his face broke into a sexy smile.

Her heart began to pound as it had never pounded before.

Courage failing her at the last, she sank down onto the corner of his bed, her hands gripping tight to the comforter.

'I woke up and you were gone,' he said.

'Had a few goodbyes to say. We go home today, you know.'

'We do. The plane's set to pick us up at four o'clock. I'm thinking we'll head off around midday and get something to eat in Launceston. I can't tell you how much I'm looking forward to getting my hands on that Porsche again.'

He *brrrrrmmmed* like a little boy, grinning from ear to ear.

Hannah felt as if she was about to faint. Her self-protective instinct told her to cut and run. To give him a bright smile and thank him for a lovely weekend. Go back to a life of pretending that she wasn't working side by side with a man who made her melt just by glancing her way.

But then he slipped his arms into a crisp white shirt and she found herself drowning in the subtle scent of soap. His skin was still slightly damp, so the shirt clung to him in places, highlighting the muscle, the might, the perfect smattering of springy dark hair on his chest. Her mouth watered so fast she was afraid to open her mouth for what might come out.

But she'd sung karaoke and survived.

She'd lost the dad she loved and survived.

She'd had enough of just surviving. She was ready to live. And to do that she needed the man who put the Technicolor in her day.

She wasn't going anywhere.

'We need to talk,' she barked.

Bradley turned to her slowly as he did up the last of his buttons. 'About?'

She lifted herself off the bed and walked to him, placing shaking hands on his chest. His warmth buoyed her, giving her wings.

'You're a good man, Bradley Knight. You work hard. And you never expect anything to be handed to you on a plate.'

'Sounds like me.' He smiled, but there was wariness in his eyes.

'But I also know that when it comes to women you've had the attention span of a goldfish.'

He laughed, surprise flaring in his eyes, before he let his towel slip, as if showing her she was spot-on.

But she knew there was more to him than that. She knew he was kind, and thoughtful, and heroic when someone he cared for was in trouble. And her heart wanted what it wanted.

She reached over to the chair and found his jeans, handed

them to him. Waited till he'd slipped them on before she said another word.

And when he stood before her, looking more beautiful than any man deserved to be in the crisp white shirt and dark jeans, and bare feet and liquid grey eyes, she took a deep breath and said, 'I've had a crush on you for the longest time. And I think I let it continue because you were so unavailable. It gave me the perfect excuse not to put myself out there for real. And then you had to go and call my bluff.'

She stopped to take a breath. Her blood pounding in her ears. Waiting for his response. Any response. But the room remained dead quiet.

After what felt like a hundred years had passed he reached past her for the light grey sweater on his bed and tugged it over his head.

She hadn't expected him to leap onto the bed and jump around whooping in excitement, but she hadn't expected this level of cool. Not after what they'd been through together. Not after the way he'd made love to her, the way he'd spooned her as they slept.

So she sucked in a deep breath, collected together every molecule of love she felt for the big lug, and without a lick of body armour stepped onto the battlefield alone.

'Bradley, you'd have to be blind not to realise that I'm in love with you, and have been—well, for ever.'

She held her arms out in supplication, then let them fall to her sides. They tingled, wanting to wrap around him. To pull him close. But he just stood there, looking through her with those impossibly impenetrable grey eyes.

Fear and excitement and anticipation came together in a great ball of emotion and she blurted, 'I just told you I love you, Bradley. I'm in love with you. I don't want to go back to work tomorrow and pretend this never happened. I want to date you, and hold your hand, and have dinner with you, and make love to you, and wake up in your arms and—'

She watched in amazement as right before her eyes he literally took a step backwards. But, worse, she saw him retreat further and further inside himself, exactly the same way he did when some effusive stranger stopped him on the street looking for an autograph.

Even while fear flooded her, she understood why. His childhood had made detachment come as easily to him as breathing. But that was just tough. No matter how deep inside himself he fled, she meant to follow.

'Bradley. Look at me. *Really* look at me. I'm opening myself up to you. Completely. Offering you everything I have to give. Because… Because we're like a pair of gloves: functional alone, but not complete without the other. I'm yours, Bradley. For ever if you'll have me.'

'Nobody can promise for ever.'

She almost wept with relief that finally he'd said something. 'I can. And I am. I know with every fibre of my being that I'm yours. Eternally. I'm not going anywhere.'

Feeling as if she might explode if she didn't touch him, lean on him, feel a response from him whatever it might be, Hannah reached out a shaking hand and laid the back of it on his cheek.

He flinched as though burned.

She recoiled as if she'd been slapped.

Feeling more scared than she had in her entire life, Hannah curled her hand into her chest and her feelings into her heart.

Oh, God. She'd screwed everything up royally. Building castles in the air with no foundation but her own woolly romantic mush for brains. Bradley didn't want her. He would never want her. Just as she'd always tried to convince herself was the case.

'This is all the response I'm to get from you?'

Silence.

A great ball of anger—most of it directed at herself for

being so foolish—built up inside her and she leapt forward and pummelled a fist against the wall.

It hurt.

Puffing, she stopped. Defeated. And furious with it.

She waved a hand across his eyes as though he was comatose—which to all intents and purposes he was. Emotionally catatonic. While she loved him enough for the both of them.

With that most ridiculous of thoughts in mind came one last shot of determination—or hope, or sheer bloody-mindedness. She pressed forward, stood on her tiptoes, slid her hands into his thick dark hair and kissed him.

Eyes closed. Heart racing.

Those lips that had burned hers, become intimate with every inch of her, brought her to the edge of ecstasy and beyond over and over again, acted as if she wasn't even there. Heat emanated from him. Soul-deep heat that told her he was wrong and she was right. Yet he remained unmoved.

Then she hiccuped, and a flood of tears poured down her cheeks. That, and the taste of salt in her mouth, woke her from her trance. *Finally*. She made to pull away.

And that was when she felt it. A softening of his lips. A response so subtle she stopped breathing.

And then he kissed her. So gently she was almost sure she was imagining it. If that was the case, oh, what an imagination she had!

Soft, warm lips brushing against hers. Tasting hers. Taking away her tears. It was a kiss so beautiful she could barely remember why she was crying in the first place.

And then it came to her. She loved him, but he wasn't man enough to even summon up a response.

She pulled away, wiping her hands over her face, across her mouth, trying to erase the sensation that felt so much like love returned when it was nothing more than a learned response.

She stumbled to the other side of the bed and leant her

hands on the bedspread. Needing space to breathe, room to think.

He didn't follow. He didn't come after her. He still didn't say a damn thing.

There was only one thing she could do.

Her voice was raw as she said, 'I can't go back to work tomorrow and pretend nothing happened. And since it's your company, and I can't convince you to be the gentleman and sell up, it looks like this is going to have to fall to me. God, I feel so predictable.'

'You're quitting?'

And that gets a response!

'You've given me no choice.'

He took a step her way and held out a hand. 'I never asked you to quit. That's the last thing I want. In fact, if I'm being honest, I'll admit it's the reason I came down here in the first place.'

He ran a hand up the back of his hair. His face was stormy.

'Things are so busy at work right now I had to be sure there weren't any inducements here that might tempt you to stay.'

'You hijacked my holiday in order to make sure I'd come back to work for you?'

Of course he had! She made his life so easy. He *liked* his life to be easy. As a move, it was so self-centred, *so him*, she couldn't believe it had never occurred to her.

Argh!

'Only now I don't know why I bothered. You're leaving anyway.'

'Excuse me? Oh, you are unbelievable. Anyone else in my position would have left months ago. But I loved the work that much, and respected you that much, I relished the long hours and hard work. While you… You push people to breaking point, then shake your head in surprise and say "I told you so" when they finally snap.'

He came around the bed. 'Hannah…'

She took two steps back, far enough away that she couldn't feel the tug of warmth from his body.

He said, 'If you think I *only* made love to you with a view to forcing you out, then you must really think I'm some kind of bastard.'

She threw out her arms in a wild shrug. 'I'm not sure what to think right now. My judgement is clearly impaired when it comes to you. Now I'm wondering how the whole "you take over the Tasmania idea" thing fits in. What was that? Some kind of payment for services rendered?'

Finally she saw some emotion in his eyes. She'd never seen him look angrier. If he was any other man she would likely have ducked and weaved. Her nerves crackled as if they'd been stripped raw.

His voice was as deep as a valley when he said, 'I only ever offered you the Tasmania proposal because you deserved it. Because I thought the subject matter would suit your style more than it suited me. And because I thought it would make you happy. I'm sorry you thought otherwise.'

He was sorry. Not that he didn't love her. Not that she was standing there feeling as if her heart had been trampled by a herd of elephants in tap shoes. He was sorry she'd *misunderstood* him.

This time even *he* couldn't make the word 'sorry' sound as sexy as he once had. This time it meant goodbye.

She turned her back on him, then realised she had one last thing to say. 'I know you think you've found a way to not let what your mother did to you shape the course of your life. But you seem determined to repeat her greatest mistakes. You shut people out. Always. And once you decide to, that's it. No room for compromise. No room for anyone.'

She didn't wait to see if he'd even heard a word of it. 'I'm going for a walk. I'll be back in two hours. Be gone or I'll have

Security throw you out of my room. I can do it, you know. I have a famously magical way with management.'

Without stopping to grab a coat or her handbag, she walked out of the suite door and took off down the hall towards the lifts.

CHAPTER ELEVEN

DAYS later Bradley sat at the café on Brunswick Street, staring unseeingly at a busker who was playing a song he couldn't put his finger on.

Like a mosquito in his ear Spencer babbled on and on about the Argentina trip. How excited he was. What he was going to pack. The vaccinations his mother had insisted he have before letting him leave the country. The fact that Hannah had organised everything so brilliantly he wasn't sure what he'd be called on to do, but he was willing whatever it might be.

'I'm sorry? What did you say?' Bradley asked, something dragging him back to the present.

'Hannah,' Spencer said, and Bradley felt the name hit him like a bullet to the chest.

Nobody had dared mention her name when he'd stormed into the office Tuesday morning with the news that she no longer worked for Knight Productions and made it clear that was the end of that.

'She did a great job of organising the trip,' Spencer finished.

Then he snapped his mouth shut, as though he'd just real-ised he'd said something wrong but wasn't sure what it might be.

Spencer's mobile beeped, and he grabbed the thing as if it

was a lifeline. 'It's the airport. I'm going to find somewhere quiet to take this.'

You do that, Bradley thought, his gaze winging back to the busker, only to find he was packing up. His disappointment was tangible.

'She hasn't found another job yet.'

Bradley flinched, his eyes sliding to the annoying sound. Sonja. He'd forgotten she was even at the table.

'Hannah,' Sonja said, in case he hadn't cottoned on. In case Hannah wasn't all he'd been thinking about while listening to the busker play.

Remembering the amazing light in her eyes as together they'd belted out that song.

Reliving the light so bright it had been almost stellar when she'd looked him in the eye and told him that she was in love with him.

Recoiling from the darkness in her eyes as she'd stormed out of their hotel room and told him to be gone by the time she got back.

'She's had offers, of course,' Sonja continued. 'They're pouring in every day. But instead she's remaining locked in her room, doing goodness knows what on her computer.'

He glared at Sonja.

'What happened in Tasmania?' she asked.

He gritted his teeth. What had happened in Tasmania had been meant to stay in Tasmania. Yet he felt as if he was carrying every minute of it on his shoulders like a beast of burden.

'She hasn't said a word,' Sonja said. 'She came home looking like she'd been hit by a bus. In fact she looks about as delighted with life as you do right about now.'

Bradley said nothing. Just stewed as the angry knot inside his gut got bigger and bigger.

'Fine,' Sonja said, throwing her hands in the air. 'You can both be stubborn and refuse to talk to me about it. But since

I'm living with her, and working for you, you *have* to talk to each other before you both drive me out of my mind with all your moping. So, whatever it is that you did to made her leave, go and apologise. *Now*. And save us all from all this drama.'

He shot her a sharp glance. 'What makes you think her leaving had anything to do with me?'

Sonja looked at him as if that was the most idiotic thing she'd ever heard in her entire life.

And the worst of it was she was right. It had everything to do with him. If he hadn't followed her, seduced her, then cast her away, she'd have come back from her holiday refreshed and ready to get back to work.

Why couldn't he have left well enough alone? If he had she'd be sitting there now, laughing with him, picking holes in his ideas, giving brightness to a day which now felt dull as dishwater.

He'd still be suffocating his attraction to her deep down inside, where it could do no harm. He'd never have known that there was someone out there who found it possible to love him. Happy days!

He shoved his dark sunglasses tight onto his nose and pushed back his chair so hard it scraped painfully on the concrete. 'I'm going to walk back to the office.' He threw the company credit card on the table. 'Look after it.'

Sonja nodded, concern etched all over her face.

'Tell Spencer I'll be back…later.'

He shoved his hands in the pockets of his jacket and took off down the street, heading he knew not where. Not a soul stopped him along the way for a chat or an autograph. He must have looked as approachable as a rabid dog.

Away from the glare of his staff, he let his mind go where it had been wanting to go all day.

Hannah.

Wham. Slam. Bam. He rubbed his fist over the spot on his chest that still ached days since he'd last exerted himself.

Losing her had put the whole office off kilter all week. She was the one who'd kept such a high-pressure environment fun. The one who'd meant staff turnover was at an all time low. The one whose work ethic had given him the room to just create, meaning he'd come up with the best ideas of his life.

Still, he'd run Knight Productions for years before she came along. The business had such momentum it would survive her loss. Intellectually he knew it would work out in the end.

Knowing it didn't stop him from missing her thoroughness. Missing the confidence with which she charmed his colleagues over the phone. The way she always had a coffee at his fingertips right when he needed one. The way she finished his thoughts.

He missed her feet on his office desk. The pen constantly behind her ear or clacking manically against her teeth. Her biting sense of humour. Her laugh. Her smile. Her mouth…

Hell.

He missed her taste. Her skin. Her fingers playing with the back of his hair. The soft flesh at her waist. The way his teeth sank into the delicious slope of her shoulder. Waking up with her warm body tucked so neatly into his.

Dammit. He missed *her*.

And as he walked up the bustling sidewalk the feelings he'd kept buried for so long refused to be smothered any longer. They pummelled at him until he felt every one in every bruised muscle. His feelings for her were so sweet, so foreign, so consuming, so deep, he knew there was only one answer.

He'd fallen in love for the first time in his life.

He loved her. He *loved* Hannah.

Of course he loved her! How could anyone not? He'd have to be pure rock not to love her lightness, her sense of fun, her kindness, her conscientiousness, and especially—most astonishingly, most unfathomably—the way she loved him back.

That was the truth. The candid, straight up, no embellishment truth.

But it didn't matter.

It would never have lasted. It was far kinder—to both of them—to cut it off before it had barely begun.

Who says? an insistent voice barked in his ear. He turned to find the source, only to find nobody was paying him any heed.

It's a fact, he continued to himself. *People are inherently self-serving. Relationships never last. They blaze to life and subsist on drama and eventually fade under their own lack of steam.*

She was right. Your relationships have never lasted because you sabotaged them before they had a chance to prove you right. Or prove you wrong.

Bradley felt his footsteps slowing as the other truths he'd always known to be firm began to wobble and crack. It hurt like hell, but he stood there and let it.

She left, he said to the voice he now knew was in his head.

You pushed her away. But she fought back. As long and hard as she could. Because she believed you were worth it. Your friendship was worth it. Your love was worth it. But any relationship has to go two ways, and you never fought for her. She couldn't leave you. You'd already quit.

His feet came to a halt. The Brunswick Street crowd spilled around him, muttering none too quietly for him to get the hell out of their way. But, considering the dressing down he'd been giving himself, it was water off a duck's back.

He'd quit her. Right when she'd needed him most. Right when she'd gathered up every ounce of strength and come to him, with her heart, her soul, her trust, her love in her hands, he'd decided it was too hard.

Yet being without Hannah was harder. Way harder.

It hit him like a sucker punch. It wasn't drama he'd been avoiding his entire adult life, it was rejection. The infernal emptiness that came of loving someone who didn't love you back. For a man who thrived on pushing himself to his physical limits, who relished any and every challenge life threw his way, when it came to relationships he'd been an absolute coward.

No more. Not this time.

He breathed in a lungful of cold Melbourne air. He could smell car fumes, baklava from a nearby Greek bakery, and best of all the thrilling hint that the greatest challenge of his life was just around the corner.

There was only one way he was ever going to know for sure.

He looked up, figured out where he was, spun on his heel and headed off with a clear destination in mind.

There was a knock at Hannah's door. She opened her mouth to ask Sonja to get it, then remembered it was the middle of the afternoon and Sonja would be at work.

She hitched up her PJ bottoms and rearranged her oversized jumper, and let her Ugg boots lead her to the door. She dragged it open to find—

'Bradley?'

Leather jacket. Jeans. Smelling of soap. And winter air. And that yumminess that was purely *him*. Her heart gave a sorry thump. She forced it to limp back to where it belonged, in a crushed and mangled mess, deep in her chest cavity.

'We need to talk,' he said.

'Do we, now?'

The fact that he'd used the words she feared had been the

beginning of the end a few days before would have been funny if she could remember how to laugh.

'Send me an e-mail,' she said, swinging the door shut in his face.

He stopped it with a determined hand. 'I don't know your new one.'

'Right.' Of course. Her old work email had clearly been deleted the same time she had. With a half-hearted wave she said, 'Then you better come in.'

She left the door open and moved to the couch, where she fell back into the over-soft cushions. She picked up a piece of cold pizza from a box on the coffee table and bit into it, as if that was far more interesting than anything he had to say.

While the sad truth was the second she'd seen his face her whole body had begun to thrum in anticipation.

'How old is that thing?' he asked, sniffing in the direction of the pizza box.

She shrugged. 'It wasn't in the fridge before I left for Tasmania, so not that old. What are you doing here, Bradley? If you're here to ask me to come back to work—'

'I'm not.'

'Oh.' Her stomach landed somewhere in the region of her knees. Maybe he was here to kick her in the shins a few times, just in case she didn't feel rotten enough.

He moved to look at a row of knick-knacks on the shelf over the fake fireplace. 'Unless you'd like to come back?'

'No.' She realised she'd said it overly loud, so softened it with a 'thank you'.

He nodded. 'You might like to know things are in disarray without you there.'

'You'll survive.'

'I know.' A pause, then, 'Sonja says you've been keeping busy. On your computer.'

She had. And she had a sudden need to tell him what she'd been working on. Maybe as a first step to dragging herself back into the light from the dark corner in which she'd hidden herself. 'I'm going to start my own production company. I'm thinking small to start with. Home-town documentaries. I think I'd have a flair for getting that kind of thing done, and done well.'

He finally turned to her, and she was dead surprised to see a flicker of something that seemed a heck of a lot like respect gleaming in his dark grey eyes.

It gave her courage. She put down her pizza and sat forward on the chair. 'So, if you're not here to beg me to come back, why *are* you here?'

He looked at the spare chair, then, sensibly deciding he'd likely break the silly little thing Sonja favoured, paced instead. 'I was hoping you might give me a chance to say some things. Things I probably should have said a few days ago.'

Heat began in the region of her toes and flowed clean to her scalp. She stood and paced herself. She didn't want to do this again. Couldn't. She could kick him out. She could...

But she needed closure on this thing if she was really going to be able to move forward. To begin her life anew. 'Fine. Go for your life. Talk.'

He looked at her a few long moments.

She tried to steady her heart again, but found she could not. He'd hurt her, but she loved him. Likely would for a long, long time. Unlikely she'd ever love anyone as deeply.

Then he shook out his hands as if they were filled with pins and needles. He was anxious. Skittish, even. She could only watch in amazement as the great Bradley Knight was reduced to a bundle of nerves in her lounge room.

It was with a strange sense of anticipation that she couldn't comprehend that she crossed her arms and waited for Bradley to say what he'd come to say.

'Okay, so here we go. I've been an independent man for a very long time. I like that I get to choose what I do on a

Sunday morning. I like that I have control over the remote. I like things to go my way.'

Big shock! Hannah thought, but she just sat on the arm of the couch and let him talk. The sooner he said whatever he'd come to say the sooner he'd be gone and she could drown herself in a bottle of wine.

'While you…' he said, waving a hand in the air as though hoping to pluck out the words. 'You're a smartass, and your family is like a walking soap opera. You're a disrupting influence.'

She blinked at him, not at all following where he was going. 'Fair enough. But I'd ask you to be so kind as to not put that on a recommendation letter in the future.'

He glanced at her, a first sign of humour in his eyes. She bit her lip.

'I'm trying to say you've been an unexpected force in my life.'

'I have?'

'From the day you landed in my office till the day we landed in Tasmania I never saw you coming. And it's on that subject that I need to ask you a favour.'

Her voice cracked as she asked, 'Which is?'

'That we leave what happened in Tasmania in Tasmania.'

His words ought to have felt like a slap upon a slap, but the sincerity in his voice, the uncertainty in his eyes, gave her pause.

'I thought that was what you'd already done.'

'I don't mean what happened between us there. I was a fool to think that walking away could ever be that simple.'

She breathed out slowly between pursed lips, willing herself not to get ahead of herself. 'Okay.'

'I mean that last day. The way I acted. The things I said. The things I didn't say. When you told me that you loved me…'

Hannah cringed, wishing he'd used some kind of euphemism. The fact that her love had been unrequited hurt as much now as it had then, even if he *had* come to make some kind of amends.

She stood and paced again.

'Hannah, I was taken by surprise. And not for the reasons I am sure *you* think are true. But because it came from you.'

'Right...' she said, while not having a clue what he meant.

'I know you now, Hannah. I know you've known loss. I know you've also struggled with rejection by someone you care for. I know that while you have a light inside of you the likes of which I've never known you are also serious, and cautious, and thoughtful. The idea that *that* woman was strong enough to put all that aside to love me...' His faraway gaze focussed back on her as he put a hand to his chest. '*Me*. A man who never let anything into his life he couldn't afford to lose. I have never, in my whole entire life, seen anything as courageous.'

Nope. No more pacing. Hannah's knees had just turned to jelly. 'Bradley, I—'

He held up a hand. He needed to finish. And, boy, did Hannah want him to.

'That's why when you told me how you felt I froze. I was so unprepared. I handled it badly. I feel ashamed even thinking about it. The look in your eyes...the hurt. I would make all of it mine if I could.'

'Bradley—' she beseeched, her phoenix of a heart beating its wings in her chest. But he held up his hand again. She bit her lip so hard she tasted blood.

'For all that,' he said, 'I'm so sorry.'

Her heart danced. Unlike the last time that word had passed through his lips, it no longer felt like a goodbye. It felt like a new beginning.

'Bradley—'

He cut her off again, clearly on a roll. She physically put her hand over her mouth.

'I know its taken me a while to be able to say it, but the truth is I now know that being my own man pales in comparison with how it made me feel when you told me I was *your* man. I only hope I'm not too late.'

He took two hesitant steps her way. Finally. Her whole body pulsed towards him like a flower to the sun.

'Hannah,' he said, his voice rough and unsure and utterly adorable.

'Yes, Bradley?'

Then, for the first time since he'd walked through her door, he smiled. A slow, sexy Bradley smile. And with a self-conscious shrug he said, 'I came here to tell you that you're the one that I want.'

The reminder of the song he'd made her sing made her laugh out loud. But her boisterous laughter fast turned to the most exquisite ache in her heart.

That was the moment he'd put himself into a position of extreme discomfort in order to give her the closure she needed on an issue that had hindered her through her entire life. *That* had been an act of love. Pure and simple. And she'd never realised.

She should have known he was a man of action, not of words. How could a man who'd never felt love know how to express it? Well, she'd just have to show him. Again and again and again. Every day for the rest of their lives.

Starting now.

She took the final two steps and took his face in hers.

'Bradley Knight. You, my gorgeous, stubborn man, are the one that *I* want. I should have known that you just needed more time. I've always been quicker to see the potential in things than you.'

At that *he* laughed. Loud, reverberating laughter that

rocked the thin walls of her old apartment. 'You are the most audacious woman I have ever known.'

She shrugged, while letting her fingers wander into the heavenly hair at the back of his neck. 'It is one of my most lovable traits.'

She pulled him to her and kissed him. Wholly, fully, showing him every ounce of love she had. He hooked a hand beneath her knees and carried her to the couch. She sank into it, and then some.

His eyes gleamed as he hovered over her. 'That thing is so soft I fear if I get on there with you I may not be able to get back out again.'

She raised an eyebrow. 'Is that a problem?'

His gaze raked over her before he moved his hand slowly up the inside of her jumper, making her curl into his touch. 'Not in the least.'

Eventually they pulled apart, their bodies a tangle of heat and sweat and the kind of joy they'd only ever seen in one another's eyes.

Bradley kissed the tip of Hannah's nose. 'I never thought I'd say the words, much less feel the feelings, my whole entire life. And then there was you. I love you, Hannah Gillespie.'

Actions could speak louder than words—but, boy, was it ever nice to hear the words anyway!

She wrapped her arms tight around him and in his ear whispered, 'I love you right on back, Bradley Knight.'

'Glad to hear it.'

'Do you want to hear it again?'

He shivered as her breath washed across his neck. 'Later,' he said, before covering her mouth with his.

Much later, as the sun set over Melbourne, they stood at the small window, looking out over an array of squat Fitzroy buildings with a glimpse of city lights twinkling in the near distance.

Hannah's back was tucked into Bradley's front, his arms around her waist, her arms on top of his. His chin leaning gently on her hair. Exactly as she'd seen her parents stand looking out over their suburban backyard a hundred times.

Happy. Nowhere else they'd rather be. In love.

'I meant what I said before,' Bradley said.

'I certainly hope so—or I wouldn't have let you do *any* of what just happened on the couch.'

She felt his laughter rumble through her.

'I was referring to when I told you that you're the one. You're it. There's never been anybody else, and I know there never will be. Fate would never be so kind to a guy like me twice.'

She slapped him on the arm. 'Better not.'

He tucked his arms tighter around her, his fingers sliding beneath her jumper to skid back and forth over her hipbones, creating the most delicious shivers in their wake.

'On that score, I have a proposal.'

At the seriousness in his voice she spun in his arms. 'Is this one I'm going to agree to?'

'I certainly hope so, because I'm fairly sure Australian law prohibits marriage between two people if one of them doesn't say "I do".'

She blinked up at him. 'I'm sorry, did you just say—?'

'You're the one,' he said, looking her right in the eye, giving her all the emotion she'd ever hoped to find in one man and then some. 'And now I've found you I don't see any point in waiting. You may as well marry me.'

Her throat was so blocked with emotion she couldn't even find the words.

'Come on,' he said finally, giving her a little shake. 'Do you honestly think we're ever going to find another living soul who would put up with either of us?'

'My man. The last of the great romantics.'

He grabbed her hand and spun her out. She laughed, and squealed so loud one of the neighbours banged something on the wall. But she barely heard it over the pure joy pumping through her brain.

He spun her back in. Their bodies smacked together, as close as two people could be while still fully clothed. Looking into his sultry dark eyes, she could barely drag breath in deep enough. And Hannah thought that if she loved him even a tenth as much in ten years' time she'd be one lucky woman.

Then, before she even felt it coming, he held her across the back and tipped her into the most fabulous Hollywood dip that had ever been.

'How's that for romantic?' he asked.

'It'll do me just fine.'

'Hannah Gillespie, will you *please* stop dilly-dallying and agree to marry me?'

'You say that while in a position to drop me?'

'Unfortunately it's not to my benefit. You already know I'd never let you fall.' He lifted her slowly back up into his arms. 'When I know what I want I go out and get it. I want you. For ever. If you'll have me.'

What could she say but, 'Yes'?

His nostrils flared as he let out a long slow breath. 'And just like that the world is back on its right axis.'

Then he kissed her slowly, gently, deeply. When she pulled away there were stars in her eyes. And rumbles in her tummy, which had been given little but stale pizza and coffee for several days and now craved a feast.

Only the fact that she knew how many days and nights she had to wrap herself around him in the future made her able to pull away. She moved into the kitchen in search of takeaway menus from the fridge.

She glanced at him, watching her from the other side of

her tiny kitchen bench. Big, bad, beautiful Bradley Knight. No longer her boss. Now he was simply her man.

Her inner imp twirled to life.

She said, 'You do realise that one day a show of yours will take on a show of mine in the ratings, and I'm going to take you down?'

Bradley grabbed the menus from her hand and threw them in the bin. He reached into her fridge for eggs and her cupboard for a frying pan. 'Is that a challenge?'

Hannah raised a saucy eyebrow. 'It's a promise.'

And somehow they never did get around to dinner that night.

Coming Next Month

from **Harlequin Presents®**. Available May 31, 2011.

Coming Next Month

from **Harlequin Presents® EXTRA**. Available June 14, 2011.

**Visit www.HarlequinInsideRomance.com
for more information on upcoming titles!**

REQUEST YOUR FREE BOOKS!

2 FREE NOVELS PLUS
2 FREE GIFTS!

YES! Please send me 2 FREE Harlequin Presents® novels and my 2 FREE gifts (gifts are worth about $10). After receiving them, if I don't wish to receive any more books, I can return the shipping statement marked "cancel." If I don't cancel, I will receive 6 brand-new novels every month and be billed just $4.05 per book in the U.S. or $4.74 per book in Canada. That's a saving of at least 15% off the cover price! It's quite a bargain! Shipping and handling is just 50¢ per book in the U.S. and 75¢ per book in Canada.* I understand that accepting the 2 free books and gifts places me under no obligation to buy anything. I can always return a shipment and cancel at any time. Even if I never buy another book, the two free books and gifts are mine to keep forever.

106/306 HDN FC55

Name _____ (PLEASE PRINT)

Address _____ Apt. #

City _____ State/Prov. _____ Zip/Postal Code

Signature (if under 18, a parent or guardian must sign)

Mail to the **Reader Service:**
IN U.S.A.: P.O. Box 1867, Buffalo, NY 14240-1867
IN CANADA: P.O. Box 609, Fort Erie, Ontario L2A 5X3

Not valid for current subscribers to Harlequin Presents books.

**Are you a current subscriber to Harlequin Presents books
and want to receive the larger-print edition?
Call 1-800-873-8635 or visit www.ReaderService.com.**

* Terms and prices subject to change without notice. Prices do not include applicable taxes. Sales tax applicable in N.Y. Canadian residents will be charged applicable taxes. Offer not valid in Quebec. This offer is limited to one order per household. All orders subject to credit approval. Credit or debit balances in a customer's account(s) may be offset by any other outstanding balance owed by or to the customer. Please allow 4 to 6 weeks for delivery. Offer available while quantities last.

Your Privacy—The Reader Service is committed to protecting your privacy. Our Privacy Policy is available online at www.ReaderService.com or upon request from the Reader Service.

We make a portion of our mailing list available to reputable third parties that offer products we believe may interest you. If you prefer that we not exchange your name with third parties, or if you wish to clarify or modify your communication preferences, please visit us at www.ReaderService.com/consumerschoice or write to us at Reader Service Preference Service, P.O. Box 9062, Buffalo, NY 14269. Include your complete name and address.

HPI1

"THANKS FOR NOT TURNING ON THE LIGHTS," Tyler said. "I'm a mess."

"Not in my book." Even in low light, Alex had a good view of her yellow shirt plastered to her body. It was all he could do not to reach for her, mud and all. But the next move needed to be hers, not his.

She slicked her wet hair back and squeezed some water out of the ends as she glanced upward. "I like the sound of the rain on a tin roof."

"Me, too."

She met his gaze briefly and looked away. "Where's the sink?"

"At the far end, beyond the last stall."

Tyler's running shoes squished as she walked down the aisle between the rows of stalls. She glanced sideways at Alex. "So how much of a cowboy are you these days? Do you ride the range and stuff?"

"I ride." He liked being able to say that. "Why?"

"Just wondered. Last summer, you were still a city boy. You even told me you weren't the cowboy type, but you're...different now."

He wasn't sure if that was a good thing or a bad thing. Maybe she preferred city boys to cowboys. "How am I different?"

"Well, you dress differently, and your hair's a little longer. Your face seems a little more chiseled, but maybe that's because of your hair. Also, there's something else, something harder to define, an attitude…"

"Are you saying I have an attitude?"

"Not in a bad way. It's more like a quiet confidence."

He was flattered, but still he had to laugh. "I just admitted a while ago that I have all kinds of doubts about this event tomorrow. That doesn't seem like quiet confidence to me."

"This isn't about your job, it's about…your…" She took a deep breath. "It's about your sex appeal, okay? I have no business talking about it, because it will only make me want to do things I shouldn't do." She started toward the end of the barn. "Now, where's that sink? We need to get cleaned up and go back to the house. Dinner is probably ready, and I—"

He spun her around and pulled her into his arms, mud and all. "Let's do those things." Then he kissed her, knowing that she would kiss him back, knowing that this time he would take that kiss where he wanted it to go. And she would let him.

Follow Tyler and Alex's wild adventures in
SHOULD'VE BEEN A COWBOY
Available June 2011 only from Harlequin® Blaze™
wherever books are sold.

HBEXP0611

Harlequin Presents®

brings you

USA TODAY bestselling author
Lucy Monroe

*with her new installment
in the much-loved miniseries*

Royal Brides

**Proud, passionate rulers—
marriage is by royal decree!**

Meet Zahir and Asad—two powerful, brooding sheikhs
and masters of all they survey. They need brides,
and marriage in their kingdoms is by royal decree!

Capture a slice of royal life in this enthralling sheikh saga!

Coming in June 2011:
FOR DUTY'S SAKE

**Available wherever
Harlequin Presents® books are sold.**

www.eHarlequin.com